Just Watch Me

JUST WATCH ME

Erin Silver

COMMON DEER PRESS

Published by Common Deer Press Incorporated.

Published in 2020 by Common Deer Press
3203-1 Scott St.
Toronto, ON
M5E 1A1

This book is a work of fiction. Names, characters, places, and incidents are either the product of the author's imagination or are used fictitiously.

Library of Congress Cataloging-in-Publication Data
Erin Silver—First edition.
Just Watch Me / Erin Silver
ISBN 978-1-988761-54-1 (print)
ISBN 978-1-988761-55-8 (e-book)

Cover Image: Catarina Oliviera S.
Book Design: Siobhan Bothwell

Printed in Canada

www.commondeerpress.com

To my boys, Ari and Josh, the funniest, most resilient kids I know. You are the reason I persevere.

Chapter 1

"**Hey internet, it's me, Simon.** Simon Rosen. Welcome to my first VideoKids post."

I stare into the camera, but my smile quickly fades as a familiar sound filters down the hall.

"You never help around here!" Mom shouts from her bedroom.

"How would you know what I do? You're never home!" Dad screams back.

I leap off my chair and shut my bedroom door. Nobody at school needs to hear that. I plop back into my seat. I'm at my desk on my computer recording my first livestreaming video for my Grade 7 technology project. These videos are a school assignment, but we're supposed to log on outside of class hours to create what our teacher calls "engaging content"—basically, videos where people share things that other kids want to watch. The site is kind of cool, I guess, and if you happen to be online while someone is creating a video, you can watch live. Viewers can post comments and the videos become interactive. Otherwise, you can watch later, kind of like a reality TV show. Not that I need any more reality TV in my life—my parents' constant fighting is plenty of drama for me. But never mind them. The point of the project is to figure out how to get the most views and likes.

I'm desperately hoping everyone is still asleep and that nobody will watch my first video in real time. With any luck, my video will be buried underneath all the other content kids in my class are likely to post today. I'm not one of those kids who likes the spotlight. I've never dreamed about being a YouTube celebrity who becomes famous for opening toys or posting embarrassing videos. I clear my throat and continue.

"It's Saturday morning, September 15, and this is where I spend most of my time."

I push my chair to the side and sweep my arm in an arc to show viewers what my room looks like. Mostly it's a mess. There's dirty laundry on the floor, my bed is unmade, and old *Star Wars* posters are peeling off the wall. Ah, well. It's too late to worry about that now. I turn back to my computer, unsure of what to say.

"I like YouTube—I mean, who doesn't—but VideoKids is school-approved because only our class has special access to our posts. On YouTube the whole world can watch, but I, er, guess you already know how YouTube works."

I realize I'm rambling a bit, and I scratch my nose—a dumb, annoying habit. Then I remember I'm streaming live. My face heats up like I'm being microwaved. "This is a lot more pressure than I thought it would be," I mumble.

The assignment is supposed to be fun, but I can already tell it's going to be torture. The thing is, we don't even get to edit our videos before they go live—we record it, and up it goes online for our class to see. This is supposed to teach us how to be organized. Our teacher, Mr. Sayo, says he's preparing us for the future and that this assignment will give us real-life experience about how to use social media responsibly. Honestly, I think creating our own livestreaming social media channel is a stupid assignment. How am I supposed to create "engaging content" when I have no clue what other kids will want to watch? I was sure I'd be struck with a genius idea when I was on camera, but maybe I should have been more prepared.

I scratch my nose again and clear my throat. I figure I may as well be honest.

"Guys, I really need an A in this class. Straight As all year, actually. Thanks to my high-ranking score in an epic game called *Rage of War*, I qualified for the Canadian Video Game Championships. They're being held in Vancouver this summer, and my parents agreed to take me if I get all As."

Now that I'm talking about video games, I'm getting so excited I nearly slide off the edge of my chair. I wriggle back into my seat and keep talking.

"The city's main sports stadium is converted into this

3

amazing battle arena where you can compete against the best players from across the country for a total of $25 million in prizes. I'm only twelve, so I don't expect to win—at least not the grand prize—but one day I will. Last year's winner won $6 million! When I'm older, I'm going to play video games for a living."

Suddenly, I'm distracted by the thump of feet stomping down the stairs. The front door creaks open, then slams shut, rattling the light fixture in my room. I flinch at the bang. My golden retriever, Meg, barks. I know what that slammed door means: Mom has stormed off after another fight with Dad. Mom is an emergency room doctor, so she'll probably camp out at the hospital. My dad is a social worker, so he'll shut the door to his home office, as usual.

While I definitely want to win the grand prize at the Canadian Video Game Championships, there's something I want more: to get my parents to Vancouver so they can fall in love again. That's where they were living when they met. They used to tell me about how "romantic" it was, with mountains and fancy hotels and stuff. My parents have been fighting so much lately that I think—I hope—a vacation to Vancouver might spark old memories. Maybe they'll hold hands like they used to, when I was little. Or share a bed again. Or even kiss. Gross as that is, it's the sort of thing parents do when they're happily married.

The livestream camera icon flashes on my screen and I realize I'm still filming. Great. I've been staring at my legs thinking about my parents. It probably looks like I have a bad internet connection.

Ping! Something hits my window. I look out to see the Mendelson twins, Jeffrey and Owen, throwing pebbles at the glass. I get up and open my window just a crack.

"Uh, excuse me!" I stammer. "That's dangerous!"

They snicker and toss another pebble my way. I shut the window, then pull the cord on the blinds. The shades come slapping down.

"Just ignore them," I mutter to myself as I sit back down in my chair.

Still, I can't help but feel rattled. Those boys are such jerks! I shake the thought of them from my head. I've got to get back to my live video. I wave to the camera. Why did I wave? That probably looked dorky. I scratch under my nose—even dorkier.

Sighing, I look down at the tip sheet Mr. Sayo handed out to help us get started. I scan the page for direction, but the white space is mostly filled with doodles: a stick man (me), a stick girl (Jocelyn), a few hearts. My heart thumps in my chest as I slam my hand down over the paper. I tug at the collar of my grey t-shirt. I scratch my nose. I breathe in and out until my heart rate steadies. I remind myself why I have to keep going: I need to get a good grade. I need to get my parents to Vancouver. I need to keep my family together. I adjust the brim of my favourite baseball cap—it has the Play Station 4 logo on it—and squint at my page. Finally, I'm ready.

"Er, so, as I've already said, I play video games. I've taught my dog, Meg, a few cool tricks. Even though I'm severely lactose intolerant, I can eat five hot Pizza Pockets in under three minutes. I guess eating five frozen ones would be more impressive, even if cheese didn't make me sick."

I chuckle, then continue. "I live in a house with my parents . . ."

My voice trails off. What else could I say that might be interesting? I tap my chin and roll my eyes toward the ceiling in thought. That my shoes are a size ten, but that I'm still waiting for the rest of my body to catch up to my feet? I shake my head no. That I do push-ups and sit-ups in my room at night, but I'm still so scrawny the Mendelson twins call me Rosie? I shake my head again. That would be TMI— too much information.

Just then, Meg prances into my room. She plops down at my feet with a thud. Meg's busy chewing something (surprise, surprise!), so I ignore her. I lift my hand off the page and take another quick peek at Mr. Sayo's tip sheet. Ah! *Who, what, when, where and why*—these are the things I should be thinking about while I livestream. I look up from the tip sheet and address the camera.

"I'm going to be shooting a series of live videos for my technology assignment, just like everyone else."

I offer what I hope is a winning smile. But now that I'm looking at an enlarged image of myself on screen, I'm not so sure I have a winning anything. I see a kid with braces, patches of raw pink skin under my nose where I can't stop scratching, and curly orange hair. How did I end up with hair this colour? My mom's hair is straight and brown and my dad doesn't have any. I readjust the cap that's covering my mop. I scratch under my nose again, then mentally scold myself. (Stop scratching, Simon!) How am I going to get through this video?

Meg growls at my feet.

"What have you got there, girl?"

I nudge her with my foot. She growls again.

"What are you chewing?"

I reach down to grab the pink fabric in her mouth, but she won't give it up. I tug harder, yanking the material from side to side to loosen it from her grip. She's got a good hold on it. I get down on my knees and wrestle her to the ground. My hat falls off and Meg lunges for it. I lose my balance and land with an *oof!* on my back, holding up the piece of fabric in the air.

"Meg! Give me back my hat!"

She dashes out the door. I plop back down on my swivel chair. What the heck am I holding? I shake out the pink material. It's very stretchy.

I pinch a corner and hold it up . . . and . . . oh no!

I hit the blinking camera icon to stop recording, but it's too late. Everyone has already seen Mom's underwear. There is no way I'll get an A for that!

Bing! An alert from my computer. I stare at my screen. Oh great! Someone from my class has watched my video, and they're commenting in real time. The blood pulses in my ears as I'm gripped with panic. Everyone will hate my video. They're going to think I'm a nerd. What if they think this underwear is mine? I scratch my nose, then place a shaky finger on my computer trackpad to read the comment.

Nice panties, Rosie, writes Jeffrey.

Standing up, I peek out my blinds. Damn it! Jeffrey and Owen are on my lawn, typing on their phones and howling with laughter. I get back to my computer just as Owen likes Jeffrey's comment with a thumbs-up emoji.

In under a minute, six more likes appear next to the comment. I bury my face in my hands. I never want to go to school again.

Chapter 2

Jocelyn and I meet on the sidewalk outside my house—red brick with baskets of purple flowers hanging from the porch. Other houses, like the Mendelson's, are sportier, with Toronto Raptors or Blue Jays flags in the windows. There isn't much traffic on my street, so the bigger kids play basketball or road hockey while the little kids cover the sidewalks with chalk. Today, they're all riding bikes or scooters to school. Jocelyn lives a few doors down and passes by on the way to Sterling Heights Public School. I'm usually happy to walk with her, but I've been dreading Monday morning all weekend. Even though it's a warm, sunny day that reminds me of summer, I feel too sick and anxious to enjoy it. It's like I have a boulder in my gut. I scratch my nose, then clutch the straps of my backpack as we fall into step. Jocelyn is talking, but I can't focus on anything she's saying.

My armpits are dripping with sweat. Did I use deodorant today, or even body spray? Very casually, I tilt my nose toward my armpit and take a whiff.

No! I got so caught up playing *Rage of War* this morning that I forgot. I'll smell bad on top of everything else. And just how many people have seen my video? I wonder. At last check, there were fourteen likes! The Mendelsons will definitely pick on me when I get to school. Those guys are evil. Best-case scenario: they'll laugh at me. Worst-case scenario: they'll tape women's underwear to my locker. My heart starts to pound even harder.

"Hello? Hello? Earth to Simon."

"Huh?" I look at Jocelyn as if I'm seeing her for the first time today. Her long, shiny black hair is tied up in a high ponytail. She's wearing a sleeveless white dress and runners. I can't help but see she has bigger biceps than me. I guess all her mixed martial arts training is paying off.

"I was just asking if you wanted to walk home together after school today, but you're not listening."

"Sorry," I mumble.

By now we've already walked the three blocks to school, and we're standing at the edge of the grassy yard. The metal gate clangs as Jocelyn closes it behind us. Kids are playing soccer and chasing each other across the field, enjoying their last minutes of freedom before the bell rings. They're in t-shirts and shorts, and their backpacks are flung all over the yard. They look like they're having fun, but I'm so not in the mood for fun.

"It's that video I made for tech class," I confess as we walk farther into the yard.

"Simon, you can't let it get to you. It was funny. You made people laugh."

"It was humiliating."

"Just act like it was your plan all along," says Jocelyn. "You need to learn to laugh at yourself."

"Ha ha ha," I say with a hint of sarcasm. "If you made a livestreaming video and got caught examining your mom's underwear, you'd be mortified, too."

"C'mon, Simon. I loved it—" she starts to say but she's interrupted.

"Hey, Rosie! Catch!"

I look up just in time to see a football spiralling full speed toward my head. It hits me right between the eyes. I stumble backwards and fall on my back.

"Ouch!" I yelp.

Jeffrey holds up his phone while Owen talks to the camera.

"And that, everyone, is how you throw a football," Owen tells his online audience.

Owen has mean green eyes and spiky blond hair, just like his brother. He's so big he could easily be wearing shoulder pads under his jersey, but he's not. He and Jeffrey are just oversized bullies. Owen keeps talking.

"On my channel, I'll be teaching you how to become an all-star like me and my brother."

I push myself up to a seated position, but I'm still seeing stars.

Jerks, I think as I rub my forehead.

Jocelyn glares at the twins, saying out loud what I'm too afraid to even whisper.

"That was so not cool!" she shouts to Jeffrey and Owen.

"Yeah?" says Owen, getting into Jocelyn's face. "What're you gonna do about it?"

My heart thuds in my chest. I should get up. Protect Jocelyn. Defend myself. Instead, I stare at Jocelyn while my mouth hangs open. The look on her face is terrifying. Her jaw is tense and her eyes flash like black diamonds. She holds up her fists. They're clenched and ready to fight. "You really want to be filmed getting beaten up by a girl?"

"I'd like to see you try."

While Jeffrey stands there like a mannequin with a phone, Owen twists his head back to shout at his brother. "Yo, bro, are you recording thi—"

But before he can finish his sentence, Jocelyn slides behind Owen and twists his arm up behind his back.

Owen squeals.

By now, a crowd has formed around us. They gape as Jocelyn gives his elbow an upward shove.

"Apologize to Simon," she says between gritted teeth.

Owen's face turns red. "Never!"

She squeezes the meaty pressure point between Owen's thumb and forefinger.

"Ooow!" he screams.

"Say sorry!" she demands.

"No!"

"Say it!"

"Sorry!" he finally sputters. "Sorry!"

Jocelyn lets go of Owen and shoves him. I get to my feet. Part of me is relieved to have a fearless friend like Jocelyn.

But a bigger part of me is humiliated. My best friend—a girl—just beat up a bully for me. This is worse than getting nailed in the head and holding my mom's underwear, combined.

And Jeffrey is still filming, so now I'm the star of two mortifying videos. Mr. Sayo said there would be consequences for inappropriate content, but there's nothing he can do about it now since it's all happening this very second.

"You're lucky your girlfriend came to your rescue," says Jeffrey, pointing a thick finger in my direction.

I ball my sweaty hands into fists. I'm angry and embarrassed and there's nothing I can do about it.

"You ruined my video, Rosie," adds Owen, pointing at me. "You better watch your back!"

I shudder at the threat. He's not serious, is he?

Jeffrey pans the crowd with his phone, capturing the whole scene even though the drama is over.

"What're you all looking at?" growls Owen. "Get lost! All of you!"

He shoos the crowd away with a forceful wave of the hand. Everyone disperses before he can single out another target.

The twins are still arguing as the shrill morning bell rings in our ears.

"My channel is ruined! Why didn't you stop recording?" yells Owen.

"You didn't yell 'Cut!' It's your fault," says Jeffrey.

"It's *your* fault! Hey! Are you *still* filming? Shut that thing off!"

I brush the dirt off my legs, then scratch my nose.

"Jocelyn, you've really gotta let me fight my own

battles," I tell her, looking down at my grass-stained runners.

"Seriously?" She puts a hand on my shoulder to stop me from walking away. I raise my eyes. Yup. She's arching an eyebrow at me in disbelief.

"You defending me makes me look like a total wimp," I say. "And Owen told me to watch my back. I'll never be able to walk home alone again. You made things worse!"

She drops her hand and sighs in frustration.

"I'm the one with the MMA training. What difference does it make if I'm a girl? And you"—she jabs her finger into my chest—"were already on the ground looking like roadkill when I stepped in."

She's right. I didn't defend myself at all. I didn't even try.

"Thanks for your help," I grumble as we head inside the school. I'm so embarrassed I can't meet Jocelyn's eye. The truth is, I'm impressed by her skill, and I think it's amazing that she's so strong, but at the same time I don't want her to think I'm weak.

"No problem," she says cheerily. She slaps me lightly on the shoulder. "Hopefully getting straightened out by a girl will keep the twins off your back."

Um, right, I think. That will do it.

We file down the crowded school hallway, trying not to step on anyone's heels.

"See ya!" Jocelyn says with a smile and a wave as she turns toward her French class. As I turn the opposite way for my own class—math with Mr. Dickerson—I feel a tap on my shoulder.

"Hey, Simon."

I turn around, still feeling off-kilter, and find myself

face to face with my overly friendly classmate, Vivian. She's wearing a headband with a big polka-dot bow on top. It reminds me of Minnie Mouse.

"I think it was so cool of you to let a girl come to your rescue in the yard just now," she says. "Not many guys would have the confidence to do that." She smiles, fluttering her eyelashes in a really weird way.

"Do you . . . have something in your eye?" I ask, confused and a bit concerned.

She shakes her head and bats her eyelashes again. I feel like she's waiting for me to say something.

"Your bow, is, ah, super stylish," I offer clumsily, desperate to put an end to this awkward discussion. "I'm sure Mickey Mouse would love it."

"Simon, how rude!" she says. "I made it myself!" Her face falls into a frown, and she turns away, flouncing toward class.

I furrow my brow and then shrug. I was only trying to be nice!

Chapter 3

Jocelyn's channel is about MMA—Mixed Martial Arts. It's becoming so popular everyone in our class tunes in on their own time to watch her live videos. She's gotten tons of likes, and kids have posted questions, too. They're asking her all sorts of things, like how she got into MMA, where she trains, and whether she wants to join WWE— World Wrestling Entertainment. That's why, for her next video, she's asked me to help her with an up-close-and-personal interview.

After school on Wednesday, we make our way to Combat Club, the dojo where she trains. Jocelyn is wearing shiny MMA shorts and a t-shirt with a dragon on the back.

It's from one of the tournaments she won. Her sensei—that's the title for her MMA instructor—is letting us use her office so we can have a quiet place to film. Jocelyn's sensei, Amy, is an ex-cop who has a purple belt in Brazilian jiu-jitsu, which takes longer to earn than a black belt in other styles of martial arts. I wouldn't want to get on Amy's bad side!

The office has a large window that overlooks the big blue mats where other kids are training. Through that window I watch the students practice their kicks, punches, and flips—things I could never do, but really wish I could. I pull my eyes away and look around the office; it's stuffed with gold trophies, medals, and framed photos. Some pictures show Amy competing in fights; others show her MMA students in action. There's even one of Jocelyn, mid-kick and sweaty, from a competition last year. I feel a rush of admiration.

We sit down next to each other on a worn-out, black leather couch, and I set up Jocelyn's phone on a tripod. Kids tend to log on right after school, and Jocelyn knows her audience is at its biggest at this time—around 4 p.m. I can see how many kids are online now: twenty-three and counting. Once we have the camera angled just right, I hit the button to start livestreaming.

"So, Jocelyn," I begin, "tell us about yourself."

Jocelyn flashes me a big toothy smile, and I grin back. It's an automatic reflex; people can't help but be happy when they're around Jocelyn. She's nice, not fake, which is why she's so popular.

"Well," she says, "I was born in the Philippines, and I have a younger brother, Timothy. When I was three and my brother was one, my mom moved to Toronto to work as a nanny."

Jocelyn's cheeks turn pink. She looks at me with shame in her eyes. I smile at her so she'll continue. I want to tell her that she and her family have nothing to be embarrassed about. Jocelyn gives me a shaky smile and continues. "My mom sent money home for us so we'd have clothes, food, and an education. After a few years, she was able to bring us to Canada. I've been here since Grade 3."

Jocelyn and I have been best friends since the day she arrived. I remember how our teacher asked me to be Jocelyn's buddy and show her around school. I ate lunch with her, played with her at recess, and helped her with her schoolwork.

As time went on, she became independent, popular, and great at MMA. I, on the other hand, got into video games and started spending more time in my room or in the basement, entering gaming tournaments and practicing my skills. I'm not what anyone would call popular, but Jocelyn and I are still best friends. Anyway, I already know her story, but some of our classmates are curious. Questions start popping up in the VideoKids comment thread, so I take my cue from those.

"Mackenzie wants to know how you got into MMA."

Jocelyn smiles at her growing audience—now twenty-six viewers! "Thank you, Mackenzie, for that great question," she says. "When my mom was a teenager in the Philippines, she got mugged. The guy took her money—money she needed to buy food for her family."

Goosebumps pop up along the backs of my arms. I never knew this before.

"When I moved to Canada, there was a dojo near our apartment, and my mom sent me there for lessons. She never wanted me to feel helpless. Now I believe in myself. I can handle anything."

I nod encouragingly. Then I gather my courage and blurt out the next question:

"Someone wants to know if you have a crush on anyone at school."

Confession: there is nobody named "someone" in Grade 7—that was *my* question.

Jocelyn squints and tilts her head to the side. Suddenly, I'm in panic mode. I can hear my heart pounding and the clock ticking. Somewhere in the room a fly is buzzing. I can't believe I just asked that question aloud and on video. What was I thinking? It must be so obvious that I wanted to know if she likes anyone!

Jocelyn's mouth falls open, but she closes it quickly.

"Thank you for the question, Simon," she finally says, "but I'm focussing on my training right now—and trying to get an A in technology class."

I sigh . . . too audibly, maybe. I quickly change the subject and look at the next question.

"Alison wants to know if you can demo a few moves for us."

"I'd be happy to," says Jocelyn. "And, Simon, I'll need your help."

"Me?" I squeak. "I'm . . . I'm just the interviewer. I'm not in the right clothes, or, or . . ."

"Oh c'mon, Simon!" says Jocelyn. She gets to her feet and reaches for my hand. "Let me teach you a few quick moves."

"Here?" I look around, determined to find any excuse not to have Jocelyn throw me around on camera. I've embarrassed myself enough already. I can't believe I didn't see this coming.

"You're right; we should move," says Jocelyn. She lifts the tripod and carries it out to the dojo area. We take off our shoes and socks. Great—I can smell my bare feet. As Jocelyn guides me to an empty spot on the mat, I pray she doesn't notice my sweaty footprint trail on the mat.

"So, let's say your attacker approaches you from the front," Jocelyn says towards the tripod and phone, addressing her VideoKids audience. She motions for me to move forward as if I'm about to attack her. "One basic move you can try in this situation is to kick the bad guy where it really hurts—like this." She demonstrates as if she's about to kick me between the legs. I instinctively cover my privates and double over to protect myself. "That will disable him and give you time to get away."

She motions for me to stand up. Reluctantly, I follow her lead.

"Another great move is to smash a bad guy in the nose with the heel of your palm, like this."

She comes at me with her hand. I duck, but in one swift movement, she manages to clutch me by the collar, kick my legs out from under me and throw me on my back. I land with a great big thwack! At first, I'm too stunned to move. Eventually, I manage to roll onto my side and curl up into a tight ball.

"And that's what happens if you can't get him in the nose," Jocelyn tells her audience. "Thank you, everyone, for your questions. Simon, thanks for the great demonstration. I hope you all keep watching. Bye for now!"

She switches off the camera and rubs her sweaty hands

off on her shorts. Then she crouches down next to me.

"Simon, I've been thinking about your situation with the Mendelson twins. You really should take a few lessons at the dojo so you can protect yourself if you need to."

"Mhmmm," I murmur, my face sticking to the mat.

"I worry about you, Simon. What if I'm not there to help you one day?"

That might be a good thing, I think. But yeah, maybe I should sign up for a few lessons, and sooner rather than later. Otherwise, I'll always be the guy curled up on the floor.

Chapter 4

Bam! Bam! Bang-bang-slap!
I'm slouched on the old plaid couch in my basement, video game controller in hand. Behind me, Jocelyn delivers a series of kicks and punches to Dad's punching bag.

Her martial arts videos have more thumbs-up emojis than any other videos in our class. I didn't say anything to Jocelyn, but I was not happy to see how many people "liked" watching her pretend to beat me up. Even Mr. Sayo was impressed.

He congratulated her in front of the whole tech class for a strategy she didn't even know existed: cross-promotion, which she achieved by appearing on Owen's channel. On top of that, kids had liked watching her over-power the school bully. Word spread quickly across the school. Now, even students in other grades high-five her in the halls. Jocelyn's a social media celebrity already. She'll definitely get an A.

If I were the teacher, I'd give myself an E for Embarrass-ing. I'm really going to have to up my game if I'm going to earn an A, too.

"Why don't you do a channel about being a gamer?" asks Jocelyn. She stops beating up Dad's bag and watches the TV screen as I pass level five of *Rage of War*.

"Woohoo!" I shout as I punch the air. Jocelyn gulps from her water bottle.

"How is playing video games a good idea for a school project?" I ask. "There are tons of streamers out there al-ready, so it wouldn't be very original. Plus, video games and school don't mix."

"But video games are your thing—you qualified for the Canadian championships. It would be so easy for you."

"It might backfire. Teachers don't approve of video games, and there's too much at stake. My parents said I need an A in every class to get to the VG Championships, remember?"

I hear my parents upstairs in the kitchen. The low rum-ble of their voices has escalated into a shouting match. I grind my teeth and try to block out the all-too-familiar sounds, focusing on the screen instead.

Jocelyn plops down beside me on the couch. Sweat is dripping down her forehead. I lean away from her and keep playing.

"I really need to get them to Vancouver," I mutter as the

front door slams shut, followed by another loud bang—the door to Dad's office. Sadly, I've memorized the sound each door makes when it slams. I guess we won't be eating dinner as a family tonight. Again.

"Don't tell me you think you can fix your parents' marriage by getting an A and going on a family trip to Vancouver." She shakes her head and gives me a skeptical look.

My hands stop their frantic movements and I stare back at her. How did she know? "Who says that's my plan?" I say defensively.

"Simon," she says, placing a warm hand on my leg. "I don't think this is something you can fix."

I don't dare move. On one hand, Jocelyn is touching me—and in a nice way, not in an I'm-gonna-kick-your-butt sort of way. On the other hand, I'm kind of annoyed. How is it possible that she can read my mind? I move my leg away and toss my controller onto the ottoman in front of us. Game over. She doesn't believe my plan will work, but I'll show her. I'll show everyone. I'll get straight As, I'll go to the VG Championships, and I'll keep my family together, too. I get to my feet and look down at her.

"Just watch me," I say.

I swivel on my heel and march toward the staircase. With a backward glance, I ask, "Are you going to help me shoot my Pizza Pocket video or what?"

Since winging it wasn't a great strategy for my first official VideoKids post, I've come up with a plan: I'm going to ward off diarrhea by popping a lactose pill, and Jocelyn will shoot me eating as many steaming hot Pizza Pockets as I can in three minutes. I might look skinny, but I have a healthy appetite. I can feel the adrenaline as it starts to pump through my body. I'm suddenly feeling super-charged, like a Tesla Model S car in Ludicrous mode. I'm ready to make cool videos and get an A in tech class.

Jocelyn follows me up the narrow staircase to the brightness of our kitchen. Meg is lying by the fridge in a patch of late afternoon sun. She looks sweet and innocent, but she's definitely mad at me for something. Why else would she have brought Mom's underwear into my room last week? Retrievers are smart, and I figure that if the Mendelsons can figure out ways to take revenge, Meg can, too.

I head straight for the fridge, but Meg won't budge from her spot. It's no wonder—this dog loves to eat, especially people food. The vet told us she's overweight and at risk of becoming diabetic, so Meg's on a strict diet. She's only allowed one cup of dry kibble twice a day. But does this stop her from trying to eat all the foods that are now off limits? Nope. Whenever we're eating, she either sits at our feet whimpering or she tries to jump on us. If food drops on the floor while Dad's cooking, Meg pounces on it before we can bend over to pick it up. When Meg is successful at sneaking food, Mom goes nuts. Sometimes she'll lecture me, Dad, and Meg for an hour at a time about dogs and diabetes and the outrageous costs of veterinary care. That's why I'm super careful with food around Meg. Now that I think of it, she's probably mad at me for not letting her eat from my plate anymore.

As I open the freezer and grab the orange Pizza Pocket box from the frozen metal shelf, Meg looks at me with a hopeful lick of her chops. I reach into the cabinet for a plate and pop five Pizza Pockets into the microwave.

Jocelyn takes a seat on a bar stool at the kitchen counter. Once again, she looks doubtful.

"Don't look at me like that," I warn. "I can eat all five in three minutes. All you have to do is film and time. Leave the hard part to me."

"Okaaay," she says, shrugging her shoulders. I know she's skeptical.

The microwave beeps and Meg is on her feet, tongue lolling.

"Sorry, Meg. These aren't for you," I tell her.

I remove the plate from the microwave with my bare hand and nearly drop it on the ground. I must have put the timer on for too long—the plate is hot as a cookie sheet right out of the oven. Jocelyn shakes her head in disapproval, but this only makes me more determined.

"You ready?" I ask. Now that my plate is safely between us, on the counter, I hand her my phone. It's already set up to record. "All you have to do is press the camera button."

"Yeah, thanks, Simon. I know how this works. I have the top-rated videos in tech class, remember?"

I narrow my eyes at her, then look down at what would be Mission Impossible for anyone else. There, in front of me, are five Pizza Pockets, with steam curling out of the flakey crust. There's hot ooey-gooey cheese and chunks of pepperoni inside. I try to smile confidently as I eye my plate. For a moment, I'm not sure this is going to be as fun and delicious as I expected. There's so much food, and it looks so hot!

"You don't have to do this, you know," says Jocelyn, giving me an out.

I won't let her have the satisfaction. I count down with

my fingers: "three-two-one."

Jocelyn hits record and nods for me to begin.

"Hi again!" I say to the camera. "Welcome to my first food challenge. You're watching history in the making as I eat five steaming hot Pizza Pockets in under three minutes."

I lift one pocket to my lips. My fingertips feel like they're blistering from the heat, but I can't back down now. Especially not on film—or in front of Jocelyn. My brain is telling me no, but I hear myself talking to the camera in spite of my better judgement:

"Ready, set, go!"

I jam a corner of the pie into my mouth and take a gigantic bite. Steam hits the roof of my mouth as sauce bursts out of the crust. My eyes sting and tears spring to my eyes. Skin is peeling inside my mouth, but I keep chewing and crying. Heat escapes from between my lips as I take a second to let out some of the burn. I feel like a dragon. I manage to gulp down the last bite of my first Pizza Pocket. Four more to go. I grab the next one. It seems to have grown in size. And was it always this heavy and overfilled? Somehow, each pocket suddenly looks like a gigantic calzone. I should have gone with the Pizza Bites!

I look up at Jocelyn with bulging eyes. Her hand is on her cheek, and she's shaking her head. Quickly, I wipe the tears from the corners of my eyes. I bite into the next pocket. My teeth feel like they've been set on fire. I open my mouth to breathe, exclaiming "Ha-ha-ha!" but the heat is too much. A chunk of pepperoni falls out of my mouth and lands with a *plop!* on the floor. Meg lunges for it, swallowing it before I can grab her by her collar.

I gulp quickly. "Meg!" I yell through all the food in my

mouth. "Leave it! Leave it!"

Mom would kill me if she knew Meg ate a giant piece of meat from my Pizza Pocket. Dad wouldn't be thrilled either, but luckily he's busy in his office.

"Leave it!" I yell again, but Meg isn't chewing frantically. She's making this weird gagging noise. That's when it hits me.

"Oh no—she's choking!"

Jocelyn and I lock eyes.

"Give her mouth-to-mouth!" Jocelyn shouts.

"Mouth-to-mouth? On a dog?"

"Yes! Mouth-to-mouth!" she screams.

My eyes are wild and I'm desperate for direction. I swallow my food with a hard gulp to make sure I don't start choking, too.

"Okay, okay! How? How?"

"Um . . . um . . . um . . . I read it somewhere—I think you have to close her mouth and breathe into her nose."

"Are you sure?" I ask, my voice high-pitched and frantic. My Pizza Pocket challenge is the furthest thing from my mind now—as is my video audience.

I had no idea you could give dogs mouth to mouth, nor does this sound remotely right, but there's no time to Google it or even scream for Dad. I get down on my knees, flip Meg onto her side and clamp a hand over her mouth. Then I cover her wet nose with my lips.

"Breathe!" Jocelyn stands over me and coaches. "Breathe!"

I breathe and breathe, thwacking Meg on the back when I run out of air. I breathe into her nose and hit her back some more. By some stroke of luck, Meg pushes herself onto her front paws and vomits. My heart doesn't restart until she upchucks the pepperoni onto the kitchen floor.

I throw my arms around my dog. "Meg," I whimper. I hold her tight and pet her shaggy coat. "You're alright." Burying my face into her golden fur, I murmur, "Meg, you're my best friend. You're everything to me!"

"And . . . cut!" yells Jocelyn as she switches off the camera.

My eyes pop open and I look at up at her. Jocelyn smiles triumphantly at me.

"Simon, that was great. You're a hero!"

Chapter 5

When I get to school the next day, Vivian is leaning against my locker. She's done away with the big bright bow in exchange for a more subtle look. The crocheted neck scarf—definitely another one of her crafting projects—looks a bit warm for September, but I zip my lip.

"Hi," I say. "Did you forget which one was your locker?" I point down the hallway helpfully.

"No, silly," she smiles. "I came by to congratulate you. You're a hero! You saved your dog."

"Uh, thanks," I answer. My face heats to the same temperature as my Pizza Pockets. I turn to my locker and fumble with my lock.

Vivian thrusts an oversized book in my face: *Caring for Your Dog: A Guide for Dummies.* I roll my eyes and take it from her. I'm hoping she'll leave, but she doesn't.

"I went through the book myself and marked the page about how to save a choking dog," says Vivian. "I also high-lighted the step-by-step instructions for how to give your dog the canine Heimlich maneuver—just for future reference."

"Huh?"

She smiles. "Giving a dog mouth-to-mouth isn't really a thing, but you're so talented it worked anyway. I also loved the way you held Meg after saving her. It really brought out your sensitive side."

Ugh, I'm so embarrassed! I desperately want Vivian to stop talking like this, but I also don't want to be mean to her. I sigh and shake my head, hoping she'll get the message. Maybe if I don't say anything she'll just go away. I shove the book into my locker and slam the metal door shut, but when I turn around, Vivian is taking out her phone.

"Do you mind if I take a few selfies with you?" she asks, flipping the camera so the lens faces us.

"Uh, yes I do mind," I tell her. She holds up the phone and throws her arm around my neck, pulling me toward her. That's when my nose starts to twitch. I let out a big sneeze. I glance at Vivian through watery eyes and realize she went way overboard with perfume. Did I mention I'm allergic to perfume, too?

I wipe my nose with my sleeve as Vivian continues to snap selfies.

I look around, horrified, and see that everyone in the Grade 7 hallway is looking at us.

"Put the camera away!" I beg. I try to pull away but she practically has me in a headlock.

"Stop!" I gasp between sneezes. I try to cover my face with my arm, but I can't react on time. My next wet sneeze sprays Vivian in the face.

"Simon!" she shrieks, finally letting me out of the headlock. Her hand flies to her cheek as she tries to wipe off the snot.

"Okay! The show's over!" says Mr. Sayo, directing his students into the classroom. "Class is now in session. Everyone take a seat. Put the phones away."

I look at Vivian apologetically as she rushes to her desk. She sits down and wipes her face again, this time with her scarf. Her expression tells me that she's still pretty grossed out.

Jocelyn sits down at the desk next to mine and giggles. "If only you could have caught that on your channel!"

I scowl at her. I know Jocelyn is only kidding, but I do feel kind of bad for Vivian. I'd never want to embarrass her or anyone else, especially on video. I know too well how that feels.

"So, we've had some really great VideoKids posts lately," says Mr. Sayo. "You all deserve a round of applause." He claps his hands, but only a smattering of kids join in. I don't feel like celebrating.

"There was Simon who saved his dog on camera," Mr. Sayo says, giving me a meaningful look. My face burns, from my orange hairline down to my grey shirt collar. "And then there was Jocelyn, who stuck up for a friend and taught us all a few self-defence moves. I'm seeing some really creative, interesting posts."

A few hands shoot up in the air.

"Yes, Patrick," says Mr. Sayo, calling on a shy kid in the back of the class. He just came to our school in September, so I don't know him well at all. I turn to look.

"Well, I, er, um, am having trouble understanding what 'engaging content' means."

Several kids in the class murmur in agreement.

"That's an excellent point, Patrick. Thank you for bringing that up."

Vivian thrusts her hand into the air. She's sitting in the front row and grunting, desperate to be picked. If I were the teacher, I'd call on her just to get her to stop.

"Yes, Vivian."

"According to the Online Marketing Institute," she says, "engaging content gives viewers something surprising to laugh at, new information, or a different way of thinking about something. It can be useful, inspiring, or entertaining. Viewers can relate to it in a meaningful way."

"Hmmm," says Mr. Sayo. He rubs his chin thoughtfully. "Very good, Vivian."

"Can I stand in the school washroom and see if anything interesting happens in there?" asks Jeffrey.

"Definitely not," Mr. Sayo says, frowning. "That would be an invasion of privacy, not to mention illegal."

Jeffrey looks disappointed.

Owen shouts out, "I'm going to teach people about sports on my channel."

"Yes," says Mr. Sayo. "Your first video in the field pushed the limit of what's acceptable, but it's a valid idea."

Owen looks smug, and Jocelyn snorts. I flash her a smile.

Henry, a geeky kid I've never really spoken to, raises his

hand. "I thought tech class would be about computer programming or something." His face turns red. "I don't like being the centre of attention."

Some kids grumble in agreement. I nod, too. Patrick and Henry have raised good points. If I wanted to be in the spotlight I'd have signed up for drama class. Or auditioned for the school play.

A knock at the door interrupts our discussion. Our principal, Mr. Burnstein, is waving through the glass panel. Mr. Sayo opens the door and ushers him in.

"Well hello, there," says Mr. Burnstein. He stands at the front of our class, hands clasped in front of him.

"Hello, Mr. Burnstein," our class mumbles in unison.

"I'm pleased to share some good news," he continues.

We all sit up straighter in our seats.

"The rest of the school has caught wind of your VideoKids project. It turns out so many students are interested in seeing your content that we've decided to open up the server to the entire student body, not just your class."

"That's great news," says Mr. Sayo happily. He reaches out to shake Mr. Burnstein's hand.

Great news? This isn't even good news. It's the worst news I've ever heard since the day we got this assignment.

Patrick raises his hand again. This time he has an even harder time spitting out his sentence. "Er, ah, so, you're, ah, saying that instead of thirty-two kids watching our videos, all 1,100 kids in the school will have access?" His voice squeaks at the end. He sounds as miserable as I feel. Even though this is the age of social media and everyone seems to want to be a YouTube star, Patrick and I have something in common: neither of us want to be one of them.

"That's exactly what I'm saying," says Mr. Burnstein. "All students and even teachers will now be able to see your work."

Mr. Sayo claps again. "This really is fantastic news. Thank you, Mr. Burnstein." He turns to the class, eyes shining. "Now you have an even larger audience with whom to showcase your creativity. What a great opportunity to enlarge your social media platform."

Jocelyn grins at me. "Isn't this great?"

No! I want to shout. It isn't at all. How am I going to get out of this now? Maybe I could petition another school to take me in on compassionate grounds? Oh! If my parents get divorced, one of them might move into another school district and I can switch schools.

I'm hit with a wave of shame—what a terrible thought. I don't want my parents to split up just so I can get out of tech class! I realize, with a sinking sensation in my gut, that whether my live channel is seen by 32 people or 32 million, I've got to find a way to make this project work for me.

Chapter 6

'm in my room at the end of a long day, about to film my next video. Maybe Jocelyn is right. Maybe I should just show my class—no, my school—how to be a whiz at video games. Kids like video games, and there's no one in my school better at playing them than I am. While other kids are busy playing baseball or hockey or doing whatever it is they do, I spend hours with a controller in my hands. I have lightning fast reflexes, I know all the cheat codes, and I keep my cool when I compete. Mom and Dad have tried to cap my screen time over the years, but I'm really smart, and my grades aren't suffering. Eventually, my parents lightened up a bit and let me spend more time gaming without giving me too much of a hard time about it. The way I see it, everyone else is allowed to choose a hobby, so why can't this be mine? Plus, these days, my parents have plenty of other things to worry about besides how many hours I spend pursuing my dreams. And now I have an even better excuse to play video games: it's for a school assignment!

It was easy to figure out how to play a game on my computer while livestreaming it for everyone else to see. In fact, it only took me three minutes to set up a split screen. If I'm going to make my fortune one day as a gamer, I might as well start today with a VideoKids channel devoted to playing video games. No more letting people into my personal life. No more being rescued by Jocelyn on Owen's channel. No more trying to impress people with how many Pizza Pockets I can eat, only to end up giving mouth-to-mouth to Meg. From now on, I'm just going to be myself and share what I know best.

I've chosen a game that's appropriate for school—one without guns, stealing cars, or beating people up for fun. Basically, you have to survive an obstacle course and make it to the next level without crashing and burning.

I shift my butt to the side and let out a squeaky fart, just to get it out of my system before I'm live. I crack my knuckles one by one, then I tilt my head from side to side until my neck cracks, too. I lean sideways again and fart one last time. It smells more than I expected, but luckily nobody watching will ever know. I hit the camera icon. I'm live on my own channel for the third time.

"Hi everyone," I say. "Today I'm going to show you how to pass this amazing obstacle course game called *Survivor*. If you're a beginner it might be tricky, but if you watch what

I'm doing, you'll definitely learn some—"

"You knew I always wanted to take ballroom dancing lessons!" yells Mom as she barges into my room, holding a neatly folded pile of laundry. "I signed us up thinking now might be a good time to try something fun together, but *noooooo*—"

Dad is right behind her. "You know I hate dancing," he says. "Ever since I was a kid and my mom signed me up for tap dancing lessons I've hated it. Why would you think—"

I gape at them. "What are you two doing in here?" I ask, annoyed.

Mom sits down on my unmade bed and pretends to pick lint off her jeans. "Just putting away the laundry, but your dad and I are having a little disagreement, that's all."

"Well I'm actually in the middle of some—"

Dad comes over and and ruffles my hair, which was already a curly mess, thank you very much. His nose twitches, and he starts sniffing like a dog. "What smells in here, Simon?" he says, his face screwing up in a mix of curiosity and disgust.

"It's probably some dirty socks or underwear," Mom says to Dad. "I always find stains in his underwear."

"Guys!" I yell.

"Are you going to pretend you're the only one who does any laundry in this house?" says Dad. "I do a load a day, and I find stains in his underwear, too."

Mom frowns and shakes her head. Then she turns to me. "Simon, your room is such a pigsty."

"No, that's not the smell of dirty socks," says Dad, still sniffing like Meg. "Simon, it's you!" He points an accusing finger at me.

Mom folds her arms across her chest and gives me a suspicious look. "Did you have dairy?" she asks. She turns to look at Dad and glares at him. "Howard, what did you put in the casserole tonight? Was there milk in it? I thought I tasted milk. I've told you a million times that Simon is lactose intolerant."

"You think I don't know he has a bad stomach? I'm the one who cooks for this family. I'm the one who packs his lunches. I know our son so well I can identify what food he ate by the smell of his farts."

"Now you're just being crude. And how dare you insinuate that you do more around the house than me? We've had this discussion enough times."

I stand up, horrified. "Guys, stop fighting. I can't take this arguing anymore!" I clap my hands over my ears. Just then, Meg prances into the room. She jumps up onto my leg. Before I can get away, she starts rubbing her body against me.

"Meg! Stop it!" I yell, but she's got her front paws wrapped around my thigh, and she's thrusting her hips back and forth.

"Howard, you said she'd stop doing that when she was spayed! It clearly didn't work."

"For your information, Harriet," shouts Dad, "she's trying to exert dominance over Simon. Being spayed takes away her ability to have puppies, not her psychosocial need to show dominance over a family member."

"Down! Now!" Mom shouts in her most commanding voice.

Meg finally puts all four paws on the ground and lies down submissively.

"At least someone around here listens to me—oh, never mind!" Mom shouts as she storms out of the room. Meg gets right back onto her feet and follows Mom out the door.

I look at Dad, dumbfounded. Things are even worse than I thought. They hate each other. It's only a matter of time before they split up—unless I can stop them.

"Simon," says Dad quietly. His cheeks, including his bald head, are pink. "I'm really sorry you had to be in the middle of all that. Mom and I are trying to work on things, but—"

"Dad," I say, holding up my hand. "You really don't have to explain. Everything is going to be okay."

"I'm not sure, Simon, and I just wanted to talk—"

"No, please, no need to talk." I say, trying to stop him before he can say the words I fear the most. "You'll see, it will all be okay."

"Well, at any rate," says Dad, "at least we cleared the air." He waves his hand through the air and chuckles at his own joke. "Get it? Mom and I had a fight and now it's not so smelly in here? When we first came in it smelled like rotting eggs. But I promise, there was no dairy in the casserole."

"I know, Dad. Thanks," I say. He leans over my chair and squints at my computer screen. "What are you working on? Is that camera light supposed to be flashing red? Were you recording something?"

Oh, no. I feel the blood drain from my face. Not again.

Chapter 7

"Okay, so you've hit a bit of a snag," says Jocelyn as we ride our bikes along the sidewalk on a Sunday morning. We're taking the side roads to the nearest Best Buy. It's about a ten-minute bike ride from home, so Dad let me go without insisting that he drive me there.

"Snag? You call that a snag?" I give her a sideways glance. I look ahead just in time to swerve around a kid riding his skateboard down the middle of the sidewalk.

"Watch it!" Jocelyn yells at the kid, but by now he's long gone. Then she turns her attention back to me.

"The video of your parents fighting was hilarious! It was like watching reality TV. I'm not sure how you got them to sound so angry, but everyone loved it. Besides, you get straight As in everything. Why are you so stressed about this class?"

I sigh.

"I was hoping this would be an easy A," I tell her, ignoring the fact that my parents weren't acting at all—that's just how they are. I'm pedalling extra hard to keep up with her pace, and I'm starting to sweat. Even though it's technically fall, it's surprisingly humid. My curly hair will be a frizz ball when I take off my bike helmet. "I thought I'd get to program a robot or fly drones. Instead we're starring in our own live social media channel. You know I hate being the centre of attention. Henry and Patrick were right about this class being nothing like what we expected."

"Well, you can't drop the course now," says Jocelyn. We get to a red light, and she extends a leg to balance herself while we wait. I pull up beside her. "You're just going to have to figure out how to succeed," she continues. "For the record, I think the GoPro is a great idea."

"You're sure you don't mind wearing it on your head for my next video?"

"We've been best friends for, like, five years, Simon. Of course I'll help." She punches me lightly on the arm.

The traffic light turns green before she can see me blush. I push hard on the pedal and get ahead of her. Her legs are strong from all her MMA conditioning. She's beside me in just a few pedal strokes. When she takes the lead, I push harder. My scalp prickles with sweat, but she's barely out of breath as we veer left into the Best Buy parking lot.

"I win!" shouts Jocelyn. She smiles at me, and for one moment I feel like the coolest guy in the world, even if I lost our little race. Her smile makes me feel like anything is possible. Even an A in technology class this semester.

We lock our bikes together on a bike rack and head inside through the automatic sliding doors. The air conditioning blasts us in the face, and I shudder from the chill. We make a beeline for the camera section. Grabbing the GoPro box off the shelf, I pay with several crumpled twenties. We're in and out in a flash. Then we head to Starbucks at the corner of the plaza.

"Can I buy you a drink?" I ask in a voice that I hope sounds mature. I hold the door open for Jocelyn, catching a whiff of her hair as she brushes past me. Vanilla and strawberries.

"Sure," she says.

Standing in line, she cranes her neck to look up at the menu board. Her forehead scrunches. "Simon, you're lactose intolerant. Is there anything you can drink here?"

"Lactose shmactose. I've got an iron stomach," I brag. Sure, I can ask them to make my drink with almond milk or tell them to hold the whipped cream, but it never tastes as good as the original. Plus, I brought a lactose pill, so my stomach should be fine.

We order our grande vanilla frappuccinos with extra whipped cream. A few minutes later, we're seated on the patio under an umbrella, where my pale freckled skin is safe from the sun. I reach into the pocket of my shorts for the little white lactose pill. There's nothing there but a hole. The pill must have fallen out on the ride over. By now, my throat is parched and my drink is sweaty. The whipped cream is starting to melt under the domed lid. Jocelyn is already drinking from her green straw. What should I do? Quench my thirst and risk a stomach ache or collapse from dehydration?

"Thanks, Simon," says Jocelyn, after taking a great big sip. "This is yummy."

Decision made. I lift my drink to my lips and take a long sip. It's delicious—sweet and frosty and refreshing.

"Bet I finish before you," I tell her.

Okay, making up eating contests doesn't really prove anything, but I really want to impress her. With all her MMA training, Jocelyn is already stronger and faster than I am. Plus she knows how to defend herself against an attacker. I'll show her I can attack this drink in record time!

My phone rings just as I'm slurping the last few drops. I pull it out of my pocket and swipe right. My grandfather appears on FaceTime.

"Hi Grandpa!" I say, waving at him. My stomach gurgles. I clutch it instinctively with one arm.

Jocelyn tilts the phone her way. "Hi, Mr. Rosen!" she smiles.

"Well, if it isn't the dynamic duo," Grandpa says. I swirl my finger around my ear while I'm off camera to show Jocelyn I think my grandfather is nuts for calling us a dynamic duo.

I adjust my PopSocket and set the phone down on the table so we can both see the screen.

"What are you lovebirds doing?"

Jocelyn giggles behind her cupped hand. My face ignites and I glare at him. I scratch my nose. He thinks he's got a great sense of humour, but this is *so* not funny.

"What? What did I say?" Classic Grandpa. Always trying to be funny when really he always just embarrasses me.

I take my hand and run it across my throat, miming for him to cut it out. Maybe my glare wasn't obvious enough.

Grandpa chuckles. "Barbara!" he yells to my grandmother. "Come here!"

We hear a shuffling in the background, then the screen freezes. We stare at Grandpa, who's been caught mid-blink.

When the screen unfreezes, Grandma appears on camera. But something is definitely not right with this picture.

"What is it Larry?" she asks, peering into the phone.

"G-G-Grandma!" I gasp. "You're not wearing any clothes!"

"Oh, hi, Simon! Hi, Jocelyn!" she says. "I didn't know you were on FaceTime. I was just about to take a shower. Larry, why didn't you tell me!" She slaps him playfully on the shoulder and moves behind him so all we can see now is her head, neck, and bare shoulders. They look like a two-headed monster.

Jocelyn stifles another giggle but I avert my eyes. I'm so mortified I want to disappear into thin air. Anything embarrassing that can happen always happens to me, guaranteed. My stomach gurgles again.

"Was that your stomach, Simon?" asks Grandma.

I clutch my stomach and wince in pain.

"Did you eat something you shouldn't have?" asks Grandpa, his face creased with concern. "You know you have to be very careful or you'll get diarrhea."

This is too true.

"I've got to go!" I shout so loudly that everyone on the patio looks at me. I'm in such a rush I don't care. I need a toilet—now!

Chapter 8

Jocelyn and I race to my house. Leaping off my bike, I drop it at the top of the driveway. I pedalled so fast I actually beat her. In my mad dash, I let out a few silent-but-deadlies, hoping she wouldn't be trapped in the cloud of smog I left behind. But I can't worry about that now. I jiggle my key in the lock and throw open my front door. Jocelyn follows me inside.

Pfft! Pfft! Pfft!

"Sorry!" I say as I accidentally break wind with each step.

What I really want is for her to go home, but I'm focussing so desperately on not having an accident in my pants that I can't get the words out. Sure, it would have been faster to use the washroom at Starbucks, but who wants to go in a public bathroom? Now I'm in a bind. As much as I want to race up the stairs, I have to clench my butt and waddle up like a penguin.

One wrong move and we're looking at a real natural disaster. I toss my Best Buy bag onto my bed and get to the toilet without a moment to spare.

"I'll just wait in your room!" Jocelyn shouts.

"Please don't!" I squeak, but she can't hear me over the sound of my bowels.

I'm clutching my stomach and grunting as an entire frappuccino—and then some—loudly exits my body. A knock on the bathroom door startles me.

"Simon? Are you okay?" It's Dad.

"I'm sick," I groan. My stomach is convulsing.

"Oh no. Sorry to hear—and I mean that literally! I just wanted to talk to you when you have a minute."

I shake my head at his joke, then squeeze them shut to focus on the task at hand. "Now's not a good time," I manage.

Pfft! Gurgle! Pfft!

"It's about me and your mom."

"Not now, Dad!"

"I just want to apologize," he continues as though he hasn't noticed that I'm on the toilet and we're shouting through a bathroom door. "I know things between me and your mom are a little strained right now, and I've been very preoccupied. I think we should spend some quality time together—just us guys—and get back on track."

"Whatever you want!" I gasp.

"No, Simon. Not whatever *I* want. It's whatever *you* want."

"I want you to leave!"

By now, I'm grunting and sweating. The fumes are getting to my head. The whole washroom is starting to spin. All I want is to be left alone. For a few moments, there's silence on his end of the door. Beautiful silence.

Then I hear Dad talking to someone—Jocelyn. Oh shoot. I totally forgot she's still here. I hope she can't hear the noises I'm making.

"What's in the Best Buy bag?" I hear Dad ask her.

"Dad, just leave it!" I shout. "It's for a school project. I still have to set it up on my computer."

"Why don't Jocelyn and I give it a try while you're in the washroom?" he shouts back.

"Leave it!" I yell again, but another wave of diarrhea hits me, and I clench my jaw tightly. That frappuccino with the extra whipped cream has really done me in. I'm cold and clammy and sweaty at the same time. I could be here for hours.

Meg paws at the door. "Leave me alone!" I holler. She sniffs under the door, barks happily, and finally leaves, her metal dog tags clinking as she goes.

Meanwhile, the sound of Dad's voice comes closer to the door. "This is really easy to set up, Simon. We'll have it connected to your computer in a second."

Dad's a social worker, not a tech geek, like me. He claims he was a Super Mario brothers champion back in the olden days when video games were first invented, but I don't exactly believe him. He's good at listening and helping people resolve their issues. I'm skeptical about his ability to set up my GoPro, but with Jocelyn's help, I'm sure they'll figure it out. Right now, I'm not in the position to stop them from trying. I make a feeble attempt anyway.

"Dad!" I warn.

Pfft! Pfft! Gurgle!

His bare, dry feet shuffle away on the hardwood floor.

A few moments later, he's back. "We've got it all set up, Simon. It's fitted to my head. We'll tighten it up when you wear it."

"Dad, not now . . ."

My stomach is clenched like a fist. "Oh my," I whimper as my bowels hoot and toot. The pain is good and bad all at once. I'm on the can for so long my legs begin to feel prickly, but there seems to be no end. I curse myself for all the events that led up to this moment. Signing up for tech class. Wanting the GoPro to get a good grade. Ordering a drink I can't have. For having a hole in my pocket and not double-checking for my pill first.

"Simon?" Dad pounds on the door. "Are you okay? That doesn't sound good in there."

"I told you, I'm sick," I shout.

Meg's back now, too. She barks on the other side of the bathroom door. I can just imagine her sitting there on high alert, wagging her tail and panting, waiting for me to emerge—something I'm not sure will ever happen.

"This GoPro is really cool. I'm shooting a video now."

"Dad! Don't do that!"

Pfft!

I might nearly be done in here, but not quite.

"Can you turn on the fan, please?" I yell to him. The switches for the light and fan are on the outside of the washroom. The bathroom light shuts off and I'm left in the dark.

"Dad!" I shout.

"Whoops!" The lights reappear, and the loud *whirrr* of the fan kicks in.

Finally I flush, but the toilet makes a choking sound like it's clogged. I stand up and look back. It is clogged. Now what do I do? I pull up my basketball shorts, wash my hands, then reach around for the plunger. It's tucked away behind the toilet.

"Simon! What's going on in there?"

"The toilet is clogged."

I wince at the sight as I jam the plunger into the bowl. I pump and pump but it's still clogged.

"Simon, let me in and I'll help you."

"No Dad, it stinks in here! I can do it myself."

"Just let me in. I can do it!"

The smell is too much to bear. I yank open the door and shove the plunger into Dad's hand. We're standing toe-to-toe in my small, stinky washroom. My GoPro is strapped to his head.

And it's blinking.

"Dad," I say very slowly. "Are you recording a video with my GoPro?"

"That's what I've been trying to tell you," he smiles. "This thing is really cool!"

My heart stops beating. Oh-no-oh-no-oh-no.

I walk very slowly down the hall into my room. It feels like I'm wading through a thick fog. I start to pray, but it's no use. Jocelyn is sitting in my chair, cheeks ripe as a strawberry in summer.

"I tried to stop him, but, but . . ."

As I approach my open laptop, I watch my worst nightmare unfold on screen, only the reality is way more terrifying than anything I could have imagined. It's like I'm floating above my computer, like what I'm seeing is happening to someone else. But, of course, it's happening to me. The livestreaming icon is blinking. Dad is vigorously plunging the toilet with my GoPro on his head and mumbling to himself as he unwittingly films my fourth live video for school.

"Oh, geez," Dad grumbles. "This is disgusting."

I hear him gasping for breath on my computer. As one of his hands leaves the plunger, I imagine he's covering his nose and mouth with the other. Then the volume picks up on my computer as he shouts down the hall. "Simon, what did you eat? This is revolting!"

A thought flashes through my mind before I crumple to the floor: Is this engaging content?

Chapter 9

On **Monday, I pretend I'm still sick,** but Dad refuses to let me stay home.

"You haven't had diarrhea since yesterday. I'm sure you'll be fine today," Dad reassures me. He sends me off for the day with a brown-bagged lunch.

I was hoping nobody would have seen the video I accidentally posted, but that's not the case at all.

"Hey, Simon! Hilarious video!" says one eighth-grader as he passes me in the hall.

Another kid slaps me on the back. "Way to go!"

While I'm putting my bag in my locker, Jocelyn comes up to me and puts her arm around my waist in a sort of one-armed hug. My breath catches in my chest.

"Simon, your video was a total hit," she says, smiling. "I'm just glad you're feeling better and that everything worked out for the best."

I turn to look at her and she blushes. I don't exactly know what it means when a girl blushes, but I get this squishy feeling inside—and not the diarrhea kind of squishy. Is it possible she likes me, and not in the social media "like" sort of way? Just as I'm about to ask if she wants to go to Starbucks some other time (for a different drink!), another kid gives me a playful noogie.

"Great video, Simon!" he shouts on his way down the hall.

Jocelyn grins at me and heads off to class. The moment has passed.

Since my channel is doing so well, at least according to everyone else, Henry and Patrick ask to come over after school for some help. They are both really shy. Patrick has a doctor's note confirming his diagnosis of anxiety. He's been excused from performing in the annual holiday concert every year since Grade 3. Henry has a support hamster in a little carrying case at all times to help with his panic attacks.

Unfortunately for us, there was no getting out of tech class once the semester began. Patrick and Henry tried to switch courses, but Mr. Burnstein told them that all the other classes were full and they'd end up having to make up for the lost tech credit in summer school. This wasn't an option for either of them. Henry goes to Scrabble camp in Boston over the summer and Patrick already has a volunteer job lined up at the retirement centre. We are all stuck having to somehow succeed on this VideoKids assignment.

"Normally, we wouldn't have asked for help with this sort of thing," says Henry as we walk along the sidewalk toward my house, "but I'm really struggling."

"Me too," says Patrick. "Henry and I are in the same boat."

"Well, not the same boat, Patrick," says Henry. "Technically we're on dry land."

"Don't worry," I tell them. "I get the point."

If Jocelyn were here we'd roll our eyes at each other and smirk, but she's filming another MMA video today before her class. It's just me and the two biggest dorks in class. I mean, I know I'm not cool, but Henry never goes anywhere without his hamster Bernie and his *Official Scrabble Players Dictionary*. Patrick dresses like the old people he helps—with his pants practically pulled up to his armpits. Despite their social status, Henry and Patrick are really nice. If I really, *really* had to name one good thing about this VideoKids project, I'd say it was how it pushed me to get to know new people. And now I get to hang out with two of my biggest fans.

"I just don't like being the centre of attention," Henry adds as we continue toward my house. "I don't even think I could manage it without Bernie in my pocket."

"My hands and armpits sweat profusely," says Patrick. "I've been diagnosed with hypodermatitis."

"Ah, good word, Patrick!" says Henry. He comes to a stop, pulls a little spiral-bound notepad out of his pocket, and scribbles *hypodermatitis* into his book. He rushes to catch up with me and Patrick.

"Is there anything you haven't been diagnosed with?" I ask Patrick.

"Good question," he says. "I don't yet have the flu, but because cold and flu season is just around the corner, I'm getting vaccinated next week. You can never be too careful when you're working with the elderly."

There's no point rolling my eyes anymore. They say so many dorky things I'll end up with a pulled eye socket.

I unlock my front door. Dad is standing there with a plate of banana muffins. "Hi, Simon!" he smiles. Henry and Patrick shuffle in behind me. Dad's face falls. "Oh hi, boys," he says. "I didn't know you were bringing friends over today, Simon. I was hoping we could chat."

"We have school work to do, Dad. Maybe later."

I snatch the plate of muffins from his hands and head upstairs. "Come on, guys," I say over my shoulder. Henry hurries up after me, Meg at his heels. Before I can reach the second floor, Patrick is asking Dad for a full list of ingredients in the muffins. A minute later, he's joined us in my room, but now he's sneezing. It doesn't take a genius to realize he's allergic to dogs.

Meg whimpers as I usher her out the door. "Sorry about that, Patrick," I say.

"That's okay," he sniffles. "I have some allergies, but the muffins seem like they're safe to eat."

"Great!" I tell him, as I stuff a muffin into my mouth.

Henry takes out his trusty notepad. "So," he says, having arranged himself in my beanbag chair. "What is the secret to making videos with engaging content?"

Patrick takes a seat at my desk and I plop down on my unmade bed. He pulls his laptop out of his bag, then holds his fingers over the keypad as I finish chewing.

"Honestly, guys, I'm not sure why anyone likes my

videos," I confess. "I'm just trying to be myself, and it turns out I'm a really unlucky kid."

"How can you say that?" says Patrick.

"Yeah," agrees Henry.

I'm completely confused.

"Have you guys seen my videos? They've all been humiliating. I even manage to embarrass myself in other people's videos!"

"You're so funny!" says Henry. "I laugh so hard I cry."

Patrick bursts out laughing. Henry joins him. It must be contagious because I start laughing, too.

"Remember the one with your mom's underwear—"

"And when you gave your dog mouth-to-mouth—"

"And when my dad filmed my explosive diarrhea!" I add.

Suddenly there's silence. Patrick and Henry stop laughing. They exchange looks. Then Patrick gathers his courage. "That was actually pretty gross," he says.

We all burst out laughing again. We laugh so hard we fall onto my floor and wipe the tears from our eyes.

"My doctor says laughter is the best medicine," says Patrick, finally recovering.

"Yeah, maybe you're right," I say thoughtfully. I get back onto my bed and sit cross-legged. "So, how can I help you?"

"I don't know what to film," says Henry.

"Well, what do you love to do? What are you passionate about?" I ask.

"Hmmm . . . Scrabble, I guess."

I mull the idea over in my mind. "You know what? I play Scrabble with my grandparents, and I'm terrible. It would be great if I could kick their butts! Maybe you could film a series of videos about how to win in Scrabble."

Henry's eyes light up. "Yeah!" he says. "I could do that."

"I'd watch it!" Patrick says, nodding in agreement. "What about me? What can I do?"

"Well, what do you like?"

"I really like old people," he says. "My grandma and I are best friends. And I volunteer every weekend at the retirement centre around the corner. It's fascinating."

"What's so fascinating about the elderly?" Henry asks. His hamster squeaks. Henry unzips the carrier and Bernie pops his tiny head out. Henry pats his furry grey head and slides Bernie back inside the ventilated case.

"The facility is really clean, so that's a bonus for me," Patrick explains. "But there are all sorts of really interesting people who have great stories to share. Just because they're old doesn't mean they're boring."

I guess I can relate to that. I'm close with my grandparents, even though they don't seem that old to me. How many old people know how to use FaceTime, even if they accidentally show up naked to the conversation?

"Why don't you do a series of interviews with old people?" suggests Henry. "You could ask them to tell stories about their lives. I'd listen."

Patrick types furiously. "That's a great idea. I can't believe I never thought about that myself!"

Henry and I smile at each other. It feels good to have friends—people to laugh with, talk to and help each other when we need it.

"Ida is a Holocaust survivor," Patrick continues. "She was liberated from a concentration camp. Twenty years after moving to Canada she ended up reuniting with her remaining family."

"Cool!" I say.

"And Victor flew airplanes in a different war. He could tell us about bombs and fighter planes and stuff."

"Great!" says Henry.

By the time Henry and Patrick go home for dinner, I'm feeling happier than I have in a while. Patrick and Henry are pretty geeky, but I guess I am, too. Who's to say there's anything wrong with that? And as much as I spend lots of time online and playing video games, it feels way better to hang out with friends in person.

Chapter 10

I **awake with a start and look at the clock,** my vision blurred. Oh shoot—it's 8:10! I can't believe I slept in so long! I'm going to be late for school.

I run my fingers through my hair to untangle it, then I pat it back down so the curls won't be too unruly. I shove my legs into a just-worn pair of jeans, and I rummage around in my laundry hamper for a long-sleeve shirt. I'm rumpled from head to toe, but whatever. I have no time to worry about my appearance today. I fly downstairs.

"Hey Simon, would you mind taking Meg out before you leave, please?" asks Dad as I'm about to grab a banana from the fruit bowl and hurry out the door. He's emerged from his office with a phone to his ear and a hand over the mouthpiece. "Sorry I didn't wake you—I'm on an important call with a client," he whispers before closing the door.

Meg is sitting at the front door pawing at the glass and whimpering, a telltale sign that she really has to go.

"Fine!" I grumble, even though it isn't fine at all.

I attach the leash to her collar, and we head out the door for a quick pee and poo.

As soon as I crack open the front door, Meg dashes outside to the front yard, nearly detaching my arm from my body. She sniffs around in the leaves that are falling off the trees and piling up on the lawn. She's got her nose to the ground and she's smelling, smelling, smelling.

"Come on, Meg," I plead. "Make a pee. Make a poo." It's what we're supposed to say when we want her to go to the bathroom. Usually the command works. But not today. Meg just keeps sniffing as if she's trying to identify each individual leaf before she chooses one to poop on. Finally she squats. A pee!

"Good girl," I tell her. "Now make a poo. Come on, Meg. Make a poo."

I let go of her leash so she can have a bit more freedom. She races around the yard, through the flower beds and back to the middle of the lawn. Back and forth. Back and forth. Nose to the ground. That's a good sign. Maybe she'll go soon. Or not. She's still sniffing out the perfect spot as I tap my foot impatiently.

A couple of Grade 4 kids walk by, hurrying to school. "Hi Simon!" they shout with a wave. Meg tries to run after them, but I grab her leash and hold her back.

If she doesn't go now I'll really be late. Then I'll have to sign myself in at the office, which will make me even later. Everyone will stare at me when I weave my way through the desks to get to my seat at the back of math class. Mr. Dickerson will look down his nose at me, and probably even give me a detention. I can't afford to stay late after school today—I have plans with Patrick and Henry. I take my phone out of my pocket. Oh geez. It's 8:20. I haven't had breakfast. I haven't brushed my teeth. And I only have 10 minutes to get to school.

Meg squats. Finally! A big pile of fresh, steaming poop. It's piled high like a bowl of self-serve frozen yogurt. I pat at my hips for poop bags but my pockets are empty. Shoot! I forgot the baggies inside. I look at the poop. I start to gag. It stinks! And it's so mushy today I'd have to scrape it off the lawn with a kitchen spatula—and there's no way Mom would be okay with that. I sigh loudly. I can't worry about this now—I'll just tell Dad to get it once he's off his call.

Just as I'm putting Meg back inside the house, I spot the Mendelson twins leaving their house two doors down. My heart lodges in my throat. I can't stand those buffoons. I usually leave early—and yes, I do that on purpose. I don't want to be late, but I also don't want to run into them on the way to school. I grab my backpack from its hook and hide behind my front door. I peek at them through the glass panel. Hopefully they'll hurry up and pass by my house. I figure that if I leave a minute after they become dots in the distance, I should be able to get to school without them noticing me.

Unfortunately, they don't seem to be in a rush. Jeffrey is holding up a phone. Owen is kicking a soccer ball and talking to the camera. Their voices are so loud I can hear them from my hiding place as they cut across my neighbour's lawn toward mine.

"Today, we're going to show you how to become a soccer star," says Owen, pausing at the edge of my lawn with his foot on the ball. "I'm going to walk across the lawn, and my brother is going to kick me the ball. I'll show you how to make the perfect header. A header is when you hit the ball with your head, for all you dummies who don't know."

The boys cackle. I grit my teeth.

Owen jogs to the other end of my lawn while Jeffrey assumes his position behind the ball.

"Ready?" shouts Jeffrey, holding up the camera.

"Ready!"

Jeffrey moves back a couple paces to get a running start. He rushes toward the ball, and just as he launches it into the air, he slips on Meg's fresh poo and falls flat on his back. The ball is now covered in brown. As it spins through the air, wet bits of poo fly off in all directions.

"Oh no," I groan as the brown-smeared ball sails through the air toward Owen.

Before Owen understands what's happening, he leaps into the air and smacks the ball with his head. The ball sails back toward Jeffrey, while poop splatters all over Owen's face.

Aside from that, it really is the perfect header.

"What's wrong with you?" Owen yells to Jeffrey, who's still splayed out on his back and covered in dog poo. "You didn't even get that on camera!"

Then he starts sniffing. "Something stinks like—"

Before he can finish his sentence, Owen wipes his forehead and looks at the brown muck on his hand. He yells out a loud string of swear words. I'm a dead man walking—er, make that running.

With two minutes until the school bell, there's no time to spare. I dash out of my house and sprint across my lawn and down the street. If I can't follow them to school, I'll have to outrun them.

"Sorry!" I yell as I take off, but I'm not really sorry at all. It was a complete accident. That was so not my fault. Meg did it—and anyway, what were those meatheads doing on my lawn to begin with?

I hear the pounding on the pavement behind me. "Rosie!" they scream. "We'll get you for this! You're going to pay!"

Believe me, I want to lie down and play dead. It would make my life easier in a way, but instead, I keep going, fast as my legs will carry me. I haven't started my MMA classes yet, but this just proves that I should stop procrastinating. My heart is thudding in my chest, my tongue has gone limp, and I'm breathing hard. And still I don't stop. I can't. It's literally life or death. I run through the gate and sprint across the school yard as the second bell rings.

The sound of their breathing—like vicious wolves—is right behind me. So is the smell of Meg's poop.

"Rosie!" they shout again.

But they're too late. I yank open the school door and bump smack into our principal, Mr. Burnstein. I've never been so happy to see anyone in all my life.

I'm safe . . . at least for now.

Chapter 11

"**P**sst!"

I'm trying to focus on Mr. Dickerson's math lesson, but a hissing sound distracts me.

"Psst—Simon!"

It's Vivian.

"What do you want?" I whisper without taking my eyes off the SMART board.

If it's not her clothes or perfume distracting me, it's Vivian herself.

"That was some video this morning," she says.

Now she's got my full attention.

"Huh? I didn't post a video this morning."

"You didn't—but the Mendelsons did. I happened to catch it live this morning on my way to school. You couldn't see much after Jeffrey kicked the ball, but all their swearing off-camera pretty much told us what happened. They got exactly what they deserved when they got covered in dog poop, but I'm really worried about you, Simon."

Mr. Dickerson has his head down as he squints at an equation in our textbook. It's a very important lesson, but now I can hardly think about math.

"What do you mean?" I ask.

On the other side of me, Henry pipes up. "If you ask me, they shouldn't have been crossing your lawn like that. They were trespassing. I just hope they don't beat you up."

"Yeah," whispers Patrick, whose desk is behind mine. I turn in my seat to face him. "You've been such a good friend and inspiration to us all. I'd really miss you. Let's hope they're just full of shi—"

"Excuse me!" says Mr. Dickerson, interrupting our conversation. "What is so important that you're all whispering when I'm trying to teach?"

I twist back around and look down at my notebook.

"N-n-nothing, sir," I sputter.

"Sorry," echo Henry and Patrick.

"Well, it's not nothing, really," says Vivian loudly. I feel her staring at me—my cue to fess up.

I keep my mouth shut.

Vivian clicks her tongue at me in disapproval, then continues on my behalf.

"Mr. Dickerson, this morning the Mendelson boys had an accident on Simon's lawn and now they're threatening to hurt him. If today is going to be Simon's last day in one piece, I think we shouldn't have to spend it in math—not that we don't like math, sir, but you get the point."

"Now, now," says Mr. Dickerson, holding up his hands to shush all thirty kids from whispering and murmuring. "Nobody is going to be harmed."

Mr. Dickerson's fingers are smudged with grey lead. He tosses his Number 1 pencil on his desk and rubs his hands. "Our school is a no-bullying zone. Signs are everywhere." He points to a poster on the side bulletin board. It clearly says no bullying—no cyber, physical, or verbal bullying.

"But have the twins even noticed the board?" asks Henry. He glances around quickly to make sure Owen and Jeffrey aren't in class. He slumps down in his seat in relief when he sees two empty desks.

A minute ago, this was just a normal day in the life of me, Simon Rosen: the twins get mad at me; they make threats; I escape; repeat. I mean, those twins have been picking on me since forever. I know the drill. But now that everyone else is worried, I wonder if I should take the Mendelson's threats more seriously. They were pretty upset this morning. Maybe more upset than I've ever seen them.

"Listen here, class," says Mr. Dickerson. "I don't like the sound of this, but I also don't appreciate exaggeration. Please work on problems one through eleven in your textbooks and I'll be back shortly. I'm going to speak to Mr. Burnstein about this. Vivian, you're in charge while I'm gone."

With that, he marches out of class. Everyone gets out of their seat and begins talking all at once.

"If this could happen to you, it could happen to any of us," says a girl named Jessica.

"Yeah, they'll just find another target once they've dealt with you," adds Steve.

I can't help it. I shudder at the thought.

"Simon, we really love your videos," says Jacob. "You've made us laugh."

"Yeah, it'll be too bad if you're not around to make them anymore," says Harper.

Great. Now that everyone thinks I'm about to be pulverized, the compliments are rolling in. I really am touched.

"Thanks," I mumble.

"Come on, everyone! Let's get back to work," says Vivian. Her hands are raised in the air as she tries to take control of the room. "Problems one to eleven, please!"

Everyone ignores her. Vivian gives up and sits back down with a sigh. They're so busy talking they don't notice when Vivian pokes me in the arm.

"Ow! What?" I ask.

She motions for me to come closer. I inch my desk toward hers until the edges of our desks are touching.

"I have a confession," she tells me.

I lean in to hear more.

"I've liked you since Grade 5."

"Really?" I raise my eyebrows high in surprise. I just thought she liked to bother me for fun.

"How did you not know? I've been trying to impress you over and over . . ."

"Uh, sorry," I shrug. I'm absolutely mortified. "I didn't realize."

The silence is so awkward I contemplate moving my desk back to where it was and pretending this never happened.

66

But then I think of something to say. "Why are you telling me this now?"

Vivian shrugs again. "I guess I figured I might as well make your last day memorable for you. Plus if I won't see you again I have nothing to lose."

"Huh," I manage. "Thanks."

"So?" Vivian looks at me expectantly. "Do you like me back?"

Oh no. Of course I don't like Vivian. I've never liked her. At least not as anything more than a classmate. I only like one person. Probably only will.

"Oh," says Vivian, looking down at her desk as she somehow reads my mind. "Your heart belongs to another girl."

"I—I'm sorry, Vivian."

"That's okay," she says. She smiles sadly at me. "I've seen enough romantic comedies to know the heart wants what the heart wants. I understand."

"Uh, thanks. That's very cool of you."

"Can I give you some advice?"

"Sure."

She grabs my hands and squeezes tight. "Tell her."

"What? I can't tell her!"

"Simon, the Mendelsons are out to get you. This might be your only chance."

I nod slightly. Then her words really start to sink in. I nod with more confidence. She's right. Vivian is right. Maybe I will tell Jocelyn. What have I got to lose? Besides my hands. I quickly pull them out of Vivian's grip.

"If there's anything I can do to thank you, just let me know," I tell her. And I mean it. It's nice to hear things from a girl's perspective.

"Actually, there *is* something you can do." She taps her cheek with her finger.

Is she suggesting what I think she's suggesting? Does she want me to kiss her on the cheek? My eyes catch the "no bullying" poster on the wall behind Vivian's head. This really could be my last day alive. I might as well give Vivian a quick peck on the cheek. It will be like kissing Mom or Grandma. She doesn't reek of perfume today, either. I scratch my nose.

Yep, I might as well.

I lean toward Vivian and purse my lips. I stretch my neck a little further. My lips hover just above her cheek. *Okay, Simon,* I tell myself. *Just do it. Go for it.*

I close my eyes and make my move just as Vivian turns her head to face me. Our lips meet ever so softly. It's just a quick kiss. Over in an instant. And it happens so fast I have to wonder if it happened at all.

Vivian smiles dreamily at me. "You're welcome," she says.

Wow. It did happen. My very first kiss on my very last day on the planet. I can't decide if I should wipe my mouth with the back of my hand or thank her. My eyes dart around the room to make sure nobody saw. Phew. They're still busy gossiping about the twins.

The classroom door opens and Mr. Dickerson bursts into the room. "Everyone, everyone, attention," he says as he claps his hands together and strides to the centre of the room. "Mr. Burnstein is looking into this matter. We take bullying very seriously in this school. You've got nothing worry about. Now, it's time for a pop quiz."

The class groans loudly. My head is spinning and I'm

tempted to put my head between my knees to stop the room from whirling. Too many things have happened in a day.

A stack of papers is handed to the first person in each row, and then we all pass the stack back until everyone has the test. As I begin the quiz, I wonder if I should tell Jocelyn how I feel. My family has been invited to her house to celebrate her birthday tonight. This could be my chance.

Chapter 12

Jocelyn's nine-year-old brother Timothy scratches his butt for the millionth time in an hour.

"Honey, stop scratching," warns their mom, Maricar. Their dad, John, gives Timothy a stern look.

Maricar turns to me and my parents. "I'm so sorry he's scratching at the table. We're here to celebrate Jocelyn's twelfth birthday, and look how we're behaving—like we're in private."

"Boys scratch themselves in all sorts of places," says Dad. "Think nothing of it."

Mom gives him a dirty look and shakes her head at him.

I look down at my plate of pancit, Jocelyn's favourite

Filipino dish, wishing I could disappear beneath the pile of noodles. Is it really necessary, I want to ask Dad, to discuss where boys scratch themselves? Seriously? And did Mom have to look at Dad like that? I don't want to be the one to ruin dinner, so I just keep eating as though Dad never said a thing and Mom never made a face.

Besides this, the evening is going pretty well. My parents have mostly put their fighting on hold for the hour. They're joking around with Jocelyn's parents, sharing the bottle of wine we brought. Later, if I can get up my nerve, I'll give Jocelyn my gift—a photo album that took weeks to put together on an online photo book app.

My mind begins to drift. I imagine giving Jocelyn the album. When she turns the pages and sees our five years of friendship spread out before her, she'll get tears in her eyes. She'll reach over and hug me. "Thank you, Simon. You are so thoughtful," she'll say. Then she'll smile at me shyly. She'll lean toward me. I'll close my eyes and lean toward her. Then
. . .

"Noooo!" shouts Timothy. "Never!"

I snap out of my daydream.

"Timothy," Maricar scolds.

"She wants to look at my bum!" says Timothy, jumping to his feet and pointing at Mom. His eyes are wild.

Mom chuckles. "Honey, I'm a medical professional and a mom. I've seen way more embarrassing things than a rash."

"Oh," says Timothy, sitting back down. "I didn't know you were a doctor."

John shakes his head and covers his face with a hand.

"Please, John, don't be embarrassed," says Dad.

"Harriet looks at Simon's—"

"Dad!" I shout. I give him an angry look and he shuts up.

"Well, if you wouldn't mind," says Maricar to Mom. "It's so hard to ask my employer for time off from work. I haven't had a chance to take him to his pediatrician."

Mom reaches out and pats Maricar's hand. "I'd be happy to take a quick look and let you know if you should make an appointment with his doctor. But you know I also make house calls some evenings. It's part of my job. Please call me anytime."

John clears his throat. "I'm so sorry, but my shift is starting soon. Malls don't clean themselves."

"We completely understand," says Dad. "We've had a wonderful time. Thank you for opening your home to us."

"Well, it's just a basement apartment," says Maricar, who shifts her gaze to John and looks at him proudly, "but soon we'll be able to buy a house of our own."

John smiles back at her. Then he gets to his feet. "Your family has been a great help to ours and I look forward to celebrating many more special occasions with you."

Everyone murmurs in agreement. John looks at my parents and adds: "I always tell Jocelyn that if she spends more time with Simon, his good grades will rub off on her."

"Yes, honey, that reminds me," Maricar says, turning to Jocelyn. "Weren't you getting your science test back today?"

We all look at Jocelyn. I know perfectly well she hasn't been doing as well in school as her parents would like.

"I, er, um . . ." Jocelyn's face turns green.

I shift uncomfortably in my seat. Mom takes the opportunity to check her phone and Dad smiles awkwardly at Timothy.

The mood suddenly shifts. Jocelyn's parents are on to her.

"Jocelyn," says John firmly. He folds his arms across his chest. "You know that as newcomers to this country we have to work hard to get ahead."

"I'm not doing poorly, exactly," says Jocelyn, laying her cutlery on her plate.

"Jocelyn Jane Tubiera—"

"It's just that I've been so busy going to MMA after school every day and we have this important tech project, so I haven't had as much time to study for other subjects." Her eyes become round and watery as she pleads with her parents for understanding.

"Jocelyn, I don't mean to lecture you on your birthday, but you've got to learn to prioritize. You've got to take school seriously," says Maricar. "Am I not right, Harriet?"

"Er, maybe this would be a good time for us to leave," says Mom.

"Nonsense," says John, turning to us. "You're the closest thing we have to family in this country. Please stay."

My parents each take a gulp of wine while John wags his finger at Jocelyn.

"Jocelyn, if you don't improve your grades you won't be doing any more of your MMA."

"Dad!" Jocelyn shouts. She slaps her hands down on the table, causing all the dishes, cutlery and glassware to shake. "You can't do this to me!"

"I can do what I like. I pay for your training. I can take it away."

"But—"

"No buts, young lady," Maricar interjects. "You are

perfectly capable of getting straight As. You're a smart girl when you put your mind to it. Daddy is right. If you don't live up to your potential we'll remove all distractions."

"Mom!" Jocelyn's chair scrapes against the linoleum floor as she gets to her feet. "This isn't fair."

"As long as you live under my roof, you'll follow my rules," says John.

I look at my parents. Can't they step in? Can't they say something? Shouldn't they disagree? Kids have rights, too, you know! And Jocelyn loves MMA. Parents shouldn't be allowed to take away the thing a kid loves the most as a punishment—especially not on their birthday!

Dad tugs at his collar, clearly uncomfortable. Mom stares at her plate, but doesn't eat.

Silence blankets the room.

"Jocelyn, we can continue this discussion tomorrow. I'll be late for work."

He bends over and kisses Maricar on the cheek. Then he kisses Timothy on the top of his head. He makes his way around the table toward Jocelyn but she shrugs out of the way. Sighing, John gathers his keys and leaves for work. It's so awkward that I'm thankful when Mom suddenly tells Timothy she'll look at his rash now. They head off to the washroom, and I follow Jocelyn as she storms off to her bedroom.

She flops down on her rumpled bed and plants her face in her pillow.

"Are you okay?" I finally ask.

"No!" she grunts.

I sit down next to her on the bed, but I'm not sure what to do next. Pat her head? Rub her back?

"My birthday is ruined," she says, her voice muffled.

"It's not ruined," I tell her. "Here."

I put the photo album next to her.

She looks up. "What's this?"

"It's for you," I say, only my voice is so squeaky with nerves I don't recognize the sound of it.

Her face lights up and I'm instantly relieved. "Thanks!"

She sits up and opens the book. She turns the pages one by one, staring at each photo for a long time before turning her gaze to the next.

"Simon," she says breathlessly. She looks up and smiles at me warmly. "This is amazing. When did you find the time to do this?"

"Oh, you know . . . between video games and stuff."

I turn away and move to sit at her desk so she won't see how happy I am that she likes my gift. As I sit down at her desk, I notice that her math notebook is open. I glance down quickly and make some mental calculations. None of her answers seem correct.

I flip to the next page and the page after that. It's all wrong. I realize that Jocelyn has been so busy with her training and helping me with my videos—plus her own videos—that she's falling behind in math.

"Uh, Jocelyn," I say cautiously. "I'd be happy to tutor you in math if you like. I think you might be a little behind."

She snaps the photo book shut. The smile disappears from her face.

"What are you saying, Simon?"

She has that fierce look in her eyes. My mouth goes dry.

"N-n-nothing. Just that you help me with my work, so I can help you with yours. That's what friends do."

"Oh, so you think I'm an idiot, don't you? You agree with my parents—admit it!"

"Jocelyn, I . . . I never said—"

"That's exactly what you're saying! My birthday is ruined. Completely ruined!"

Jocelyn throws herself down on her bed and turns her face away from me. My photo book falls to the floor with a thump.

I stare at the discarded book and fight the tears welling behind my eyes. The conversation is over. I leave her room as quietly as I can. As I head down the hallway past the open bathroom door, I see Timothy, pants bunched around his ankles, bent over touching his toes while my mom examines him.

This was definitely not how I expected the night to end.

Chapter 13

Thankfully, Jocelyn and I put her birthday fiasco behind us pretty quickly. (I sent her a text message that night apologizing for hurting her feelings. She replied with a heart emoji and told me how much she liked the album.) Even though we've moved on, I definitely won't mention math to Jocelyn again. Instead, we spent hours on FaceTime last night comparing data and congratulating each other on our success. Yes, I should have been practicing my gaming skills, and Jocelyn should have been studying for her math test today, but we couldn't help getting excited.

Call it beginner's luck, but Jocelyn and I might both get an A in tech class. Despite the fact that I've humiliated myself in nearly all of my videos—and on other channels, too—my project is going well. In fact, Jocelyn and I have nearly the same number of views, likes, and comments. It's unbelievable. If I get an A in tech class by the end of the semester, I'll be one A closer to the VG Championships and saving my family. If Jocelyn gets an A and keeps her average up, she'll be allowed to continue her MMA training.

We grin at each other as we strut into tech class after lunch. It's become our favourite class now that we're getting a handle on how to create our own individual brand of "engaging content."

"Take your seats please, everyone. There's no time to waste," says Mr. Sayo. He's standing at the front of the class banging a ruler on his desk.

Jocelyn and I exchange confused looks. Mr. Sayo usually has a smile on his face and a joke on the SMART board. There are no smiles today.

Everyone files in and sits down. Mr. Sayo remains quiet until a hush falls over the room.

"I have some news I need to share with you today. Some of you will like what I have to say and others won't. It's nothing personal, but it's important."

We all start whispering to each other until the room is filled with murmurs. Is he cancelling the project? Are we in trouble for something? Is he quitting his job or gravely ill?

"Class," he says sternly, "settle down."

We quiet down again, but now I'm squirming in my seat. Jocelyn is nervously rolling her pen between her palms.

"When we originally started out on the VideoKids adventure, I wanted you to explore what engaging content means in the world of social media today. I hoped you'd learn to take it seriously and use it responsibly. I wanted you to take a chance, to come out of your shell, so to speak, to learn to plan and think on your feet. I was hoping you'd all get an A. But it's a dog-eat-dog world out there. If you work in social media or marketing, only one company's pitch gets the account. Only one company gets hired to handle a major ad campaign."

I glance at Jocelyn, but she's staring straight ahead, concentrating on Mr. Sayo's every word. At the front of the class, Vivian is biting her nails. Even the Mendelson twins are sitting straight up in their seats, their big heads and broad shoulders nearly blocking my entire view of the SMART board.

"I've been in touch with the executives at VideoKids," Mr. Sayo continues. "They're very interested in our project and have asked me to choose a single student who will receive a special prize at the end of the semester. That is why, this semester, they have asked me to give out only one A to the most deserving person."

I gasp. Jocelyn covers her mouth. A chorus of "No fair!" and "C'mon" echoes around the room. Even Henry is upset. He's been working so hard on his channel. His content has improved to the point that even I watch his Scrabble videos and comment on his posts.

Mr. Sayo lets us voice our disapproval before raising his finger to his lips to silence us.

"I know this is hard to hear," he says, "but it's an important life lesson, and I can see why the higher-ups at VideoKids have made this request. You can't all have the most popular channel. You can't all have the most engaging content. Only one of you will earn an A in this class."

Jocelyn raises her hand, but before she's called on, she shouts out her question anyway. "But sir, Simon and I are tied. We have almost the same number of views and likes. Anyone who earns it should be allowed to get an A."

"I understand, Jocelyn, but this is how things work in the professional world, and since VideoKids made this recommendation, we feel it's important to accept it."

Vivian shouts out the question that hasn't yet fully formulated in my mind. "But Jocelyn and Simon are best friends." She twists in her seat to look at us. I recognize the look of pity on her face before she turns back to Mr. Sayo. "Are you pitting them against each other as competitors?"

Jocelyn and I look at each other, eyes wide with shock. Vivian is right. That's exactly what this means. Only one of us can get an A.

But wait . . . I'm not that kind of person. I don't want to beat my best friend. It's completely unfair. The worst part is, we both desperately need an A. I shut my eyes to block out the commotion and squeeze my head with my hands. I have to think. I quickly sort out the facts in my mind. If Jocelyn gets the A and brings up her average, her parents will be happy and she'll get to continue her MMA training. If she doesn't get an A, she might have to quit the one activity she loves most in the world.

However, if I get an A, I'll get to play in the VG Championships in Vancouver. And most importantly, my parents will fall back in love on our trip. They'll realize all their fighting was pointless and they'll come home happy. I won't have a broken family. I won't have to shuffle back and forth between two homes. My life won't be carved up between two people who no longer like each other. I won't have to worry about how each of my parents will manage on their own. If I get the A, I'll save my family. In fact, I might be doing Jocelyn a favour as well. Shouldn't Jocelyn be focussing on her grades? Maybe her MMA training is too much of a distraction. If she gets a B, she'll have more time to focus on academic success.

When I open my eyes, I've made a decision.

I turn to Jocelyn with sad eyes. "I'm sorry," I whisper. "I need the A more."

Jocelyn presses her lips into a thin, hard line, the way she does when she's super angry. She shakes her head at me ever so slightly.

"We'll see about that," she hisses.

Her chair falls to the floor as she stands up and storms out of class.

Chapter 14

Back at home, I stare blankly at my screen. My VideoKids account is set up and ready to go. Unfortunately my mind is a big black hole. I have no idea what to film. I just can't think. Ever since Mr. Sayo announced there would only be one A and I told Jocelyn *I* needed the A more ("We'll see about that!" she said coldly), things haven't been the same.

I've lost my appetite. Even the thought of food makes me sick. I sprinted home right after school instead of waiting for her in our usual spot. I couldn't deal with the possibility of running into Jocelyn on our walk home. I'm so upset I can't even play video games.

I'm just not interested in anything anymore.

I glance at the clock on my screen. I've been sitting here slumped over at my desk for three hours. I've done absolutely nothing. But I can't seem to do anything else but worry.

The worst part is, I miss my best friend. And it's only been a few hours. I want to rewind the clock and go back to this afternoon when everything was normal. After tech class, she'd have gone to math, and I'd have gone to gym.

"Good luck on your test," I'd have said. And I'd have meant it.

We'd have met up after school and walked home together. We'd talk about my video games or her MMA or laughed about whatever silly thing happened at school today. Something is always funny when we're together.

Instead, I ran home by myself just to avoid the awkwardness of seeing her. I had to crouch down and hide between the garbage and recycling bins at the side of my house for a few minutes so I wouldn't walk into the house too early. The smell between the bins was horrible, and I covered my face with the sleeve of my jacket to protect myself from breathing in the fumes. I swear I could smell a week's worth of Meg's dog poo in there! Then, at just the right time—the time when I'd usually get home—I walked through the door.

"How was your day?" Dad asked. He took my backpack and hung my jacket in the closet.

I smiled widely. Maybe too widely. "Great, thanks, Dad!"

Dad narrowed his eyes. He was definitely on to me.

"I'm just going upstairs to play video games," I told him. It's what I would've usually said and done if my life hadn't been turned upside down.

"Okay," he said finally, his suspicion dispersing. "I'll be in my office if you need me."

He must be caught up in his work because it's now 6:30 p.m.—thirty minutes past our usual dinnertime—and I haven't heard from him since.

As I'm pondering all this, Meg saunters into my room and lays at my feet. Just the girl I wanted to see. I scratch her soft furry head. She rolls onto her back for a belly rub. How silly was I to think she was upset with me because I can't give her treats and people food anymore? She loves me no matter what. Meg is my one true friend.

My mind wanders back to Jocelyn. She was my one true human friend before Henry and Patrick came along. And now I'll never know if Jocelyn and I could have somehow, one day, been more than friends. Over the last few months, I've imagined new scenarios. I pictured asking her to the movies as more than just friends. I could see us holding hands in the hall and having everyone stare at us in admiration. I think we'd make a good couple. Besides that quick peck with Vivian, which I don't think counts, I never even got to experience a real kiss. By the time I get to know another girl the way I know Jocelyn, I'll probably be twenty years old. That feels like an eternity.

Maybe this whole situation should be a relief. I wouldn't know how to kiss even if Jocelyn wanted to. I move over to my bed and grab a pillow.

"Meg, what do you think?" I say, even though I know she can't answer. Nor would she have any advice about the subject if she could talk. She's lost interest in me and is pawing at a toy on the floor. She's batting at it with her paws and licking it. Typical Meg behaviour.

I get back to my pillow. I've seen kissing scenes on TV before. The couple usually whispers something to each other first. Then they close their eyes and purse their lips. Slowly, they get closer and closer until their lips are touching and their hands are around each other.

Since I'm alone in my room, I figure I'll try it out. For research purposes.

I hold my pillow up and close my eyes. "Oh Jocelyn," I say aloud. "Can I kiss you?"

No, no, that sounds silly. Are you supposed to ask for permission or just do it? I shake my head at myself. I'll just try it again.

"Oh Jocelyn, kiss me!"

I close my eyes and bring the pillow to my face. Then I smush my face into the softness of the pillow and make kissing noises. I move my head from side to side.

"No no, that can't be right," I murmur, whacking the pillow against my bed. "That's dumb."

I don't think I've seen anyone move their head around that much. And it's usually not so loud. Geez, this is hard. How will I ever learn? I decide to give it one last try before Googling "how to kiss" online.

I might as well figure it out now that I'm onto the topic. You never know how much advance practice you need before it comes in handy. After all, it's taken me countless hours to become a master at video games.

I hold up my pillow and start again. I imagine I'm looking at Jocelyn's face instead of my faded old *Star Wars* pillowcase.

I can picture her big, brown eyes and smell the scent of her strawberry-vanilla shampoo in her hair. I remember how she sort of hugged me the other day, how she blushed and smiled at me. Maybe she does like me, I think. Since it's just me alone in my room, I lay it all out on the line. I decide to be brave. To be honest.

"Jocelyn, something has changed this year. I feel it, but I don't know if you feel it, too. We've been best friends for so long, but now I get nervous when you come over. I get butterflies in my stomach when you smile at me. I'd do anything to impress you. And even though I was embarrassed when you defended me and when you wrestled me in your video, I like how strong and skillful you are. If you don't like me in that way, I understand. But the truth is, I like you as more than a friend. I will always be your friend, but if you wanted to be more, that would be good, too."

For some reason I'm nervous. My mouth gets dry. My hands are clammy. I guess this is what it feels like to be in love. Oh my gosh. I'm in love with Jocelyn. It hits me like, ah, well, like a football in the head. Except in this case, I'm scared and excited at the same time. I've never felt this way before. I decide to press on with my full confession. I'm not quite done talking yet.

"Jocelyn, I want to hold your hand in school. I want everyone to know we're going out. I want to hug you sometimes. And if it's okay with you, I'd really like to kiss you."

This is the moment I've been waiting for. The moment where we both close our eyes, and I pull her in close, and I stick out my lips and she sticks out hers and we press our lips together. Slowly, as if brought together by a magical, magnetic force, I bring the pillow to my face and kiss the girl of my dreams. After a few moments it's over and I let out a great big sigh of happiness.

"Woof!"

The spell is broken. I look down at Meg. She's batting my GoPro with her front paws. That's weird. What happened to her toy?

I'm trying to make sense of the situation but my brain isn't working. One second Meg is playing with a toy, and the next thing I know, she's using my GoPro and it's lit up as though it's recording. An electric jolt zaps through my body.

"Oh Meg," I say. "You didn't!"

Chapter 15

I'm scrolling through the VideoKids Frequently Asked Questions page desperately trying to find out how to delete a live post from the site. So far everything I've read says it's not possible, but I've got to get that kissing video offline. Maybe I'll email the VideoKids president and beg for help. Maybe Mr. Sayo will have mercy on me and cancel the whole project. Maybe there's a way to shut down the internet!

I'm sweating and sick to my stomach at the same time. And the comments from kids in my school are popping up one after the next. My screen is filled with likes and emojis and comments. I've never seen anything like it.

"Great video!" writes a kid named Joe.

"Hilarious!" writes Helena.

"I'll show you how to kiss," says Vivian.

Barf rises up in my throat.

Mr. Sayo gives me a thumbs-up emoji. I gulp. Clearly he's not going to help.

Before I can scroll through all the comments, there's a loud banging on my front door.

"Dad!" I scream. "The door!"

I don't have time to see who's there. I keep reading as the comments pour in. The banging persists, only now it's louder. It's like someone is trying to kick it down.

"Dad!" I scream, but Meg is at the door and barking so loudly I can't hear myself think. There's no way Dad will be able to hear me over the ruckus.

I race down the stairs and fling the front door open wide. A cold gust of wind hits me in the face. But it's the sight of Jocelyn that chills me to my core. I barely recognize her standing there in her MMA shorts and a t-shirt. It's nearly zero degrees outside tonight and it's already dark. She must be freezing. But I'm not about to let her in. Her hands are balled into tight fists. Her hot breath is coming out in puffs. Gone is her big smile. Her eyes are empty of warmth. It's all been replaced by a look of fury I've only seen on *Animal Planet*. My teeth start to chatter. I've never been so scared in my life.

My instinct is to shut the door in her face, but when I try, she holds out her hand and shoves the door back open.

"Simon! You have some explaining to do!"

"I—I—"

She bursts through the door, grabs my arm and drags

me into the living room. She throws me onto my couch and paces back and forth in front of me while I try to spit out an apology. I'm completely trapped. That was an accident, I want to say. I mean, yes, I do want to kiss you. Yes, I do like you as more than a friend. But I never meant to broadcast it across the whole school. Instead, I can only manage a few pig-like squeaks.

"You know what, I don't want to hear your stupid excuses," says Jocelyn. "How dare you post a video like that. Not only have you made a joke of our friendship, but you deliberately humiliated me to get more likes on your channel. You used me to beat me and get an A. The A that I need more."

No! None of that is true. It's not true at all. I want to tell her it was all an innocent mistake, but something she said brings me to my feet.

"You need an A more? Is that what you said?"

"I think you heard me," says Jocelyn.

We're toe to toe, nose to nose. I can see the fire in her eyes. Only now there's fire in my eyes, too.

"If I get the A, I'd be doing you a favour," I tell her. "You've completely lost track of what's important here. Your grades are dropping, and you spend more time doing MMA than anything else. You want to teach me MMA, but you won't even let me help with your schoolwork! Plus your parents have done so much so you can make a success of yourself. Isn't that why your family came here to begin with? How will you do that if you flunk out of school? You think you're John Cena or The Rock?"

There. I said it. It all sounds horrible, but it's the truth.

Jocelyn jabs me in the chest with a finger. "You think

you need the A? You already get straight As. You don't need this one. What? You think you'll win the video game championships and be a millionaire? You think that's a career your parents will be proud of? I bet there's some other video game nerd who plays even more than you do, who practices harder, who is better and will beat you in the end."

I clench my fists until my nails pinch my palms. "Is that what you think of me?" I shout. "That I'm a video game nerd? A loser? Someone who can't even win at the only thing I'm good at?"

She looks down at her feet. Her voice falters. She lowers her hands to her sides. "That's what I think, Simon," she says. It's barely a whisper but I heard her loud and clear.

"I think you'd better leave," I tell her, and point to the door.

"I'll leave, but I want you to know our friendship is over."

"Good," I say. "I didn't want to be your friend anyway."

"Yeah," she says softly. She looks up at me. There's sadness in her eyes. "I got that from your latest video."

I hang my head in shame. In fact, I've never been so ashamed in my life. Not when Meg chewed Mom's underwear or when the twins threw a football at my head. Not even when I had diarrhea and Dad filmed it with my GoPro. None of it compares to how awful I feel right now.

"By the way," adds Jocelyn pausing at the front door, "I'm fed up with you being intimidated by how good I am at MMA, just because I'm a girl. And if you think a trip to Vancouver could save your parents' marriage, you're wrong."

I lift my head to stare at her.

"Kids don't save marriages. That's just fantasy."

She closes the door behind her and heads out into the dark. I'm left standing in my living room in complete shock. Did all that just happen or is this some sort of nightmare? I can't believe the things she said. I can't believe what I said. How did our friendship—no, my entire life—suddenly explode like this?

I sink into the couch, my legs shaking too much to support my weight.

Maybe Jocelyn is right: I am a loser. An orange-haired, brace-faced wimpy loser.

"Simon?" says Dad, coming out of his office. "Was that Jocelyn's voice I heard? Tell her to stay for dinner."

"No thanks, Dad," I say sadly. "I don't think that's a good idea."

I shuffle up to my room and lie in bed for the rest of the night.

Chapter 16

"**Hi everyone.** For anyone new to my VideoKids channel: my name is Jocelyn."

I'm sitting in my grandparents' wallpapered living room while Grandma and Grandpa clean up from dinner in the kitchen. As I wait to start our game of Scrabble, I sit on their couch and watch my ex-best friend Jocelyn's latest live video on a tablet.

She is so angry about my kissing post—and about the things I said to her afterward—that she's fighting back online. Somehow, my one accidental video is being used by Jocelyn to launch a girl power movement at our school. I never meant to embarrass her or make fun of her in any way. It was just a private daydream gone awry, sort of like everything else in my life. I would never even have had the guts to hold her hand. But now my fantasy has become a nightmare.

"If you're tuning in, you probably already saw a video by someone who shall remain nameless," Jocelyn continues.

Great! She can't even say my name. I'm like Voldemort in Harry Potter!

She's filming from her dojo—I recognize the setting instantly. A few days before our fight, I'd signed up for MMA lessons at Combat Club because I want the confidence to stand up to any bully, any time. I feel ashamed when I remember how Jocelyn accused me of being jealous of her MMA skills. Now, with my tablet in front of me, it looks to me like she's ready for a fight. As I watch, I have to admit I'm a little afraid. But as much as I want to turn off my tablet, I can't look away.

"This person I won't name embarrassed me online. He said he wanted to kiss me. Even mocked what that would be like. On his channel! But you know what, guys and girls? You don't have to take that from anyone. Nobody gets to embarrass you in front of your classmates. No-body gets to make you feel small!"

Suddenly the camera pans to a group of girls who are shouting and cheering for the camera. Jocelyn is getting them all riled up. I scan their faces and even recognize several girls from school—including Vivian! Things are so bad that the girl who admitted to having a crush on me now wants to crush me.

The girls get in an orderly row and the camera focuses on Jocelyn. She's at the top of the mat about to teach the group some self-defence moves.

"Hi-ya!" yells Jocelyn. She breaks a block of wood with her bare hand.

"Hi-ya!" everyone echoes as they punch the air.

"Hey, what are you watching?" asks Grandpa. He eases himself down on the couch next to me. I try to cover the tablet with my hand.

"Nothing!" I squeak.

"Hi-ya!" shrieks Jocelyn again.

Shoot! I forgot to turn off the volume. Grandpa can hear the whole video.

"Lady troubles?" he asks knowingly. It's like he can read my mind.

"How'd you guess?"

"Well, you and Jocelyn always come for dinner and Scrabble together, but tonight you're here and she's, well, there," he says, motioning his head toward the tablet. I look down at my lap and turn off the device.

"Want to talk about it?" Grandpa asks.

"What do you know about women? You've been married for, like, forty years."

He chuckles. "I know more than you might think," he says. "Try me."

I'm silent for a minute. Then I blurt it all out. Grandma brings in a big bowl of fluffy white popcorn, and my grandparents are riveted as I tell them about my life. Grandma perches on the armrest of the couch and tosses popcorn into her mouth absentmindedly. They don't even interrupt once, which is probably a challenge for them.

I start from the beginning. I tell them about my tech class and how I keep embarrassing myself online, only instead of people hating me, I've somehow found a way to create engaging content. I'm sort of popular at school, except with the Mendelson twins, who have threatened to kill me. Yet of all the people who do like me, I've managed to offend the one person who matters most. I tell them about our fight and how not only is Jocelyn not my girlfriend, she's not even my friend.

"Mom and Dad fight so much, it's no wonder I don't know how to have a relationship," I finally conclude.

Grandma and Grandpa look at each other. It's like they know something I don't, but I'm too upset to bother asking.

"Simon," says Grandma, "relationships are hard. When you're older you'll understand more, but for now, I want you to know that both your parents love you no matter what."

"I'm probably the reason they fight so much. My room's a mess, I play too many video games . . ."

"Oh, come on now," says Grandpa in his don't-be-silly voice. "You're the best thing that ever happened to your parents."

"And to us," adds Grandma.

"But don't tell your cousins," Grandpa warns. "They won't be happy."

That makes me smile. I don't have any cousins.

"Your secret is safe with me." I say, smiling at them, but it's just a sad half-smile. It's all I can manage tonight.

"How about we kick your butt in Scrabble?" says Grandpa.

"I'd like to see you try," I tell him. "Just let me use the washroom first."

I get off the couch. I have pins and needles in my foot, so I limp off down the hallway to the washroom, my tablet tucked under my arm.

As soon as I'm on the toilet, I log back into VideoKids and click on the link to Jocelyn's channel. The video is over and the comments are streaming in. I scan them quickly.

"Girl power!" writes Jessa in Grade 8.

"Thanks for the demo," writes Danny from fifth grade.

Jocelyn's video even gets a thumbs-up emoji from three different female teachers at our school.

My heart feels like it's sunk to the bottom of the toilet bowl. How am I supposed to go on like this? All the girls are upset with me. Jocelyn seems to hate me.

I click on the "comment here" button. I'm about to type a simple message: I'm sorry.

A knock on the bathroom door rattles my nerves.

"Honey, are you okay in there?" calls Grandma.

"You're not having diarrhea again, are you?" asks Grandpa.

I roll my eyes. "I'm fine!" I tell them.

Shutting off the tablet, I get off the toilet and wash my hands. I'm not in the mood to play Scrabble. My grandparents will enjoy winning.

Chapter 17

It's been one week since my big blow-out with Jocelyn and her rebuttal video. Despite how much I embarrassed myself yet again, my kissing video was a huge hit. All of a sudden I'm really popular in school. Kids crowd me in the halls and ask me for advice about starting their own VideoKids channel. Students I don't even recognize tell me I'm hilarious. Plus, Vivian and Henry are making googly eyes at each other, which means she's finally off my back. On top of all this, I was completely shocked to find out from Mr. Sayo that my VideoKids kissing post was the most watched in the company's history. (In other words, since last year.)

But what should be a good week has instead been the worst week ever. When Mr. Sayo shared my record-breaking news in class, Jocelyn stood up and left. Her eyes were red when she came back. She hasn't said a word in class since then. I haven't seen her in the halls or walking home from school either. She must be avoiding our usual route.

Since I signed up for classes at Combat Club, I've been hoping to see her at the dojo so I can apologize. Every time I've been for a session, Jocelyn hasn't been there—but then again, I'm in the beginners' class, and she's more advanced. I wish I could show her how much self-defence I've learned in such a short time. I'm even practicing in the basement. I've got a good jab, hook and cross hook, and can deliver a pretty mean roundhouse kick. Those muscles I'd been hoping for are finally making their debut. I flex in the bathroom mirror every night. My biceps aren't as hard as Jocelyn's, but I'm sure they're bigger than they were before.

We got our mid-term report cards today. I'm getting As in everything but tech—we were all given the letters TBD since only one of us will get an A at the end of the semester. I wanted to text Jocelyn and tell her about my grades, but then I remembered I can't. Things should be looking up, but without Jocelyn to share it with, there's no point to any of it. I thought I'd be scared to run into her, but instead I just feel sad when I don't.

I'm biking home from another MMA lesson as the sun sets. They sky is orange and purple, and the air smells like Halloween, even though it's still a week away. My stomach is grumbling for dinner as I make a right turn and pedal down my street.

"Hey, Rosie!" shouts one of the Mendelson twins as I get closer. They're shooting another sports video on the road in front of my house. I honestly don't know when they became so mean. I've overheard my parents talk about how Mr. Mendelson is "too rough" with them. I don't know what that means—especially since I rarely see their parents at all. Mostly, Jeffrey and Owen are left to their own devices.

I think back to how we used to play together in Grades 1 and 2. They'd make me be the goalie and shoot pucks at me. Once we played hide and seek; I crouched in the bushes for hours, but they never bothered to find me. Another time we played cops and robbers; they were the cops, and they handcuffed me to the railing on my front porch with these plastic toy cuffs. I was stuck there until Mom came home from work. Mom was so mad she marched right over to the Mendelson house and banged on the door. Their dad opened it, filling the entire doorway with his body. He just shrugged his big, meaty shoulders and chuckled. "Boys will be boys," he said.

Mom left in a huff after telling him her boys were no longer welcome at our house. Eventually, I got even smarter. If they were outside, I'd go inside. Unfortunately, they're sporty. No matter the weather, they'd be outside playing one thing or another—football, soccer, hockey. I began staying inside most of the time. It's a big part of why I started playing video games. But now isn't one of those times when I'm inside.

"We're doing target practice," shouts Owen to me as I pedal closer toward home. "And guess what? You're the target."

Jeffrey spirals a football at my head but misses.

The ball bounces on my driveway just as I pull up to my garage.

They snicker at me.

I balance myself on my bike and put one foot on the ground. "Why are you always picking on me?" I shout at them from across the road. "What did I ever do to you?"

I'm so angry and fed up that I finally have to ask.

"You're a nerd," yells Owen. "And you've ruined my videos too many times. I'm practically failing tech class because of you. And then you booby-trapped your lawn with crap. I told you I'd get you for it."

They're standing shoulder-to-shoulder on the edge of my driveway. Jeffrey is filming, and Owen has his arms folded tightly across his chest. In just a few steps they could walk up my driveway and slam my face into the asphalt. If that happens, I'm doomed. But neither of them makes a move.

"Toss the ball back," says Jeffrey.

I know I can't throw a ball like they can. And even if I could, I'd have to be an idiot to throw it back to them just so they could whip it at my head again.

I climb off my bike and open the garage door with the keypad. Rolling my bike into the garage, I lean it against the wall.

"Come on, Rosie," Owen taunts. "Throw it back."

The garage door closes behind me. My heart pounds in my chest. I look at the football at my feet. I look back at them. No. I can't do it. I'm not going to throw it back to them. They'll get my wimpy throw on film. I'll just go into the house without saying a word. I'll be calm and mature. They'll have no one to pick on if I'm inside. I leave the football where it is and walk very slowly up the stone pathway toward my door. My legs are shaking and my knees threaten to buckle. Keep walking, I tell myself. Keep walking.

Thwack. One of them throws a baseball at my back. And it really hurts. That will definitely leave a bruise. At least I'm at my door now. I feel for the key in my pocket. I put the key in the lock. I have my hand on the knob when one of the twins yells the unthinkable: "We'll just ask your girlfriend to fetch the ball for us. I hear her parents like to clean up after everyone."

The boys cackle as if they're the funniest, cleverest people in the world.

I swivel around to face them. That was the last straw.

Before I can control myself, I charge down the driveway. I plant myself right in front of the twins. I'm breathing hard and my heart is pounding. Owen raises his hand and slaps me hard across the cheek.

Something inside me finally snaps. I give Owen a shove and kick the phone out of Jeffrey's hands. It bounces on the grass and lands face up on the road. I hold up my fists, ready to fight.

"Hey! If you break my phone you'll have to pay for it!" scowls Owen.

"You can take your broken phone and shove it up your—"

Before I can complete my threat, Owen comes at me with his fists. I duck out of the way, narrowly avoiding a strong right hook. I take my palm and smash him in the nose, just like Jocelyn showed me. There's a crack, and then blood spurts like a shower head.

"Oh, no!" gasps Jeffrey. "You broke his nose!"

He swings at me. Misses! I kick him in the crotch. Jeffrey collapses on the ground, groaning and clutching at his privates.

"Yeah?" I yell at the twins, who are both moaning in pain. "Who's the tough one now? Huh? Huh?"

My pulse is racing and I'm feeling stronger and better than I've ever felt before. I throw my fists in the air like a champion and dance on the spot, using some of the footwork I learned in my last MMA class. Ha ha! This feels good. You know what would feel better? Doing a victory dance like one of my avatars after passing a level of *Rage of War*. I frantically swish my hips from side to side. Then I get my arms moving, too, swinging them back and forth across my body while I move my hips. I'm flossing. Oh yeah. Look at me! Look at me! I'm flossing it out. I finally kicked their butts.

I'm so engrossed in my victory dance that I fail to notice a dark shadow rising from the ground. Out of nowhere, one of the twins comes up from behind. He kicks me, and I fall flat on my face. Then he grabs the back of my head and smashes my face onto the ground. My forehead cracks Owen's broken phone screen. It's the last thing I hear before I black out.

Chapter 18

I crack open my eyes, but everything is blurry. My head is pounding. My face feels numb. What happened to me? Why do I hurt so much?

I open my mouth to speak, but the sound of my voice is garbled.

"Thank goodness! You're up!" says Dad. He's sitting beside me and squeezes my hand. Harriet, look!"

Mom appears at my bedside.

"Where am I?" I want to say, but I can't.

"Shhh, don't try to talk," says Mom. She's in her white doctor's coat. She takes her stethoscope and listens to my chest. Does this mean she's at work? Am I in the hospital?

"What ha—" but that's as far as I get. My voice sounds broken. I'm completely exhausted.

"You were in a fight last night," says Mom. "You have a concussion, you've cracked some teeth, and you have stitches in your mouth. You've been out for over 12 hours."

I hear her, yet I don't understand. My head hurts, but I try to think back. What's the last thing I remember? Think, Simon, think . . .

"Those boys are bad eggs," says Dad, shaking his head. "I'm going to have a word with their parents."

"Or the police," says Mom. "What they did to Simon was a crime."

Crime? What happened? It feels like someone is beating my brain with a hammer, but I force myself to remember. I was coming home from MMA on my bike. It was getting dark. I was hungry. Then something hit me in the head. That's right! One of the twins threw a ball at me. I argued with them. Then they said something rude about . . . about . . . about Jocelyn! I confronted them. My cheek stings as I remember how hard Owen hit me. Then I fought back. They were down on the ground. I did the floss dance. Then . . . blank.

I wince in pain. Dad holds a straw to my broken face and I take a sip. Apple juice dribbles down my chin and wets my hospital gown.

"Hello?"

That voice sounds familiar. Jocelyn! The curtain slides back on the rod and there she is, rushing toward me.

"Simon! You're awake! I was so worried."

She throws herself at me and I groan in agony.

"Gentle," says Mom. "He's very banged up."

"Owen and Jeffrey are jerks. They should be punished for this," says Jocelyn through gritted teeth.

"How do you know what happened?" asks Dad. His face contorts in confusion.

"It was on the VideoKids channel. The twins were shooting a video when they started a fight. Jeffrey live-streamed the whole thing."

"Howard—there's proof!" says Mom, sounding excited.

But Dad is as puzzled as I am. "How is this possible?" he asks.

Jocelyn explains the whole thing. The tech project. Our videos being broadcast to the entire school. The pressure to be awarded the one single A. Jocelyn tells them how the twins blamed me for ruining their videos and how they vowed to get me back. She even told them about our fight and the unkind words we said to each other as we fought for the top grade.

I had completely blocked that part from my mind. Jocelyn and I are in a fight. We haven't spoken in ages. It's been terrible.

"I'm sorry," I croak. My voice is hoarse, but I get out the words. If it's the last thing I ever say, I will apologize to Jocelyn for the mean things I said to her. For embarrassing her online, even if it was by accident.

She turns to face me, her eyes wide and apologetic. "No, Simon, I'm sorry. I said some mean things, too. I just wanted to keep doing MMA so badly. There was so much pressure. I lost sight of what's important."

Does she mean me? I want to ask her, but I can't. I close my eyes and rest.

"Oh God, Howard. I feel terrible," says Mom, her voice shaking.

Someone is crying. Maybe it's Jocelyn. Maybe Mom. Most likely Dad.

"Mr. and Mrs. Rosen," says Jocelyn, her voice strong. "I want you to know how brave Simon was to stick up for my family the way he did. He defended me when they were putting me down, and he got beaten up as a result. It's all my fault."

"It's not your fault, Jocelyn," says Dad. He sniffles. (So, it *was* Dad crying.)

"Well, it's not over yet," says Jocelyn. I open one eye when I hear the fight in her voice. Oh no—what's she going to do? Get them in the dojo somehow? Fight them in the street? This is not good!

"We all saw what the twins did, which means we have evidence," she continues.

"Yes, Howard, Jocelyn is right. We should march into the principal's office tomorrow and get those bullies expelled."

"Harriet, you're not thinking clearly," says Dad. "Those boys live two doors down from us. It will just make them angrier, and they'll hurt Simon again."

"Oh, Howard, have some courage," says Mom.

Both of my eyes pop open.

Jocelyn shrinks into the background.

"Stop," I groan. "Don't fight."

Dad pats my hand. Mom looks down at her rubber work shoes. The guy in the next bed farts. I couldn't possibly feel any worse.

"Mr. and Mrs. Rosen," says Jocelyn, stepping toward the

bed. "I'm trained to fight, but this is a fight we won't win with physical violence. I'd like to speak to the principal myself."

"That's very brave of you, Jocelyn," says Mom, "but—"

"I think we should let Jocelyn handle this," Dad tells Mom, finding his voice. Then he faces Jocelyn. "My car is parked out front. School is in session and I'm sure the principal is there. I'll drive you to school and you can pay Mr. Burnstein a visit. We can call your parents on the way to let them know what's happening."

"Oh, Howard," says Mom, anxiety creeping into her voice. "I have to finish my shift, and I want to keep an eye on Simon. Please let me know what happens."

Mom rushes around my bed and embraces Dad. It's sort of an awkward hug. They're probably very out of practice. Even I can see that with blurry vision, but it's progress. Jocelyn smiles at me and I try to smile back. I can feel the drool escape from the corner of my mouth, but I'm too tired to be embarrassed.

Those boys are a menace. If they did this to me, they'll do it to someone else, too, someone even more defenceless than me. And I put up a pretty good fight. They've got to be stopped. If anyone can help, Jocelyn can. I close my eyes and drift to sleep.

Chapter 19

When I wake up several hours later, it's dark outside and my hospital room is filled with voices. Everyone is talking in hushed tones, but I can somehow feel the bodies in the room. I lift my eyelids and take a peek. I don't believe what I see. There are my parents and Jocelyn, Jocelyn's parents and Timothy. Grandma and Grandpa. Mr. Sayo is there, and so are Patrick, Henry, Vivian and even Mr. Dickerson. I glance around the room. I seem to have been moved to a private room—there are no curtains around me. Nobody is farting. Whoops! Except me.

All eyes turn in my direction. "Simon!" everyone seems to gasp at the same time.

I manage to sit up. "Hi," I grunt. Progress.

Jocelyn comes forward. "Simon, we don't have good news."

"The incident with the twins didn't happen on school property," explains Vivian, "so technically Mr. Burnstein can't suspend the Mendelsons for what they did."

"We failed you, Simon," says Jocelyn.

"Those guys pick on kids all the time," says Henry. "How hard could it be to catch them doing it on school property?"

"You're right," says Jocelyn, while everyone murmurs in agreement. "Just leave it to us." She flashes me a big smile. She looks confident. In control. Jocelyn.

The room erupts in excited conversation. I can't make sense of what they're saying, so I rest some more. The pounding in my head has subsided and the IV is gone. I yawn as widely as I can manage. I'm so drowsy.

I wake up late the following afternoon feeling better. The sun is shining through my window, and I wince from the brightness. I haven't seen a sunny day in I don't know how long.

Dad is snoring in a chair. His clothes look rumpled. His face is unshaven. How long has he been sitting here? He snorts suddenly and sits up. Noticing I'm awake, he breathes my name. "Simon . . ."

He gets to his feet and gently eases himself down on the corner of my bed so he won't hurt me. "How are you feeling?"

I take stock of my body. My head doesn't hurt. It feels rather clear, somehow. My mouth doesn't feel as bruised.

I can even open my eyes. And talk!

"I'm okay," I say. I sit up in bed. "Is there any food?"

Dad's face lights up. "I brought you your favourite: Pizza Pockets! And a lactose pill. Mom said it was okay, so I heated some up this morning before I came back to be with you." He rummages around in a bag for the items.

I remember my Pizza Pocket video and groan quietly. Louder, I say, "Thanks, Dad!" He seems so happy I'm hungry that I don't want to disappoint him. I take a bite of a lukewarm Pizza Pocket and chew. Actually, it's not bad, especially now that I can enjoy them without filming.

"What happened with the twins?" I ask after I've eaten two Pizza Pockets.

Dad smiles at me. "Well, you have some pretty clever friends—and tons of them."

"Really?" I ask. "What did they do?"

By the time Dad finishes filling me in, my head is spinning. I'm not sure if the concussion symptoms are back or whether I'm just overwhelmed with the news. Basically, everyone was on high alert and worked together to catch the twins in action. It didn't take long.

Vivian happened to have been wearing a particularly elaborate outfit, and Jocelyn filmed the twins making fun of her in class—which is verbal bullying.

Then, in gym class, Patrick accidentally ruined a video the twins were filming about basketball. One of the twins was demonstrating a layup, and Patrick sneezed so loudly it distracted him from making the shot. The ball bounced off the backboard and didn't go in.

The boys were so mad that one of the twins pushed Patrick to the ground. He fell so hard he bruised his coccyx bone (that's the bone at the top of your bum, apparently). Patrick's butt hurt so much he needed to sit on a cushion for the rest of the day. Vivian happened to catch that incident on her phone. Physical violence on school property was strike two.

Then at lunch, Jocelyn posted a video on her channel about how she was struggling in math. The twins went online and added their two cents. They told her she was an idiot and made fun of her parents. Again. That was strike three: cyber bullying.

This afternoon, dozens of students gathered outside Mr. Burnstein's office and made their case. It was easy to do since it was all caught on film. Mr. Burnstein had no choice but to suspend both boys from school. But then Mom and Dad showed up with my medical information. Dad told Mr. Burnstein that it was a matter of time before what happened to me happened to someone else on school property. He threatened to go to the police if greater action wasn't taken immediately. Mr. Burnstein lifted the suspension and issued an expulsion. All the students cheered when the news got out.

Of course, the twins were mad, but their parents were even angrier—though not at anyone else; they were mad at what their kids had done. I was surprised to hear that by the time my parents got home there was an apology letter from the Mendelsons waiting at my doorstep. In the letter, the boys said they were sorry for picking on me and everyone else. Their parents called mine to apologize for not taking their kids' behaviour more seriously. They also promised to make sure this would never happen again. After reading their letter and thinking about everything that's happened,

I realize that while their family life probably isn't perfect, nobody's is. I don't know why the twins have always been such bullies, but maybe—just maybe—there's a chance that even they can change.

I look down at the letter in my hands. Everything seems so unreal. Is this a dream? Am I actually awake? I'm about to ask Dad if someone is filming all of this for a reality TV show when another voice interrupts.

"Knock knock," says Mom. She comes into the room with her clipboard and doctor's coat. This must be real if my own mother is checking my pulse again. "How's my favourite patient?"

"Getting better," I tell her. "Mom, thanks for everything." I look at both her and Dad and feel a rush of emotion. Impulsively, I tell them, "I have the best family in the world."

My parents exchange looks. Now neither of them can meet my eye. Suddenly I'm confused. They're hiding something.

"What is it?" I ask, panic rising in my body. I feel my heart gallop in my chest.

"Shhh," says Mom, placing a firm hand on my forehead. "This can wait."

"No," I say. "It can't. What is it?"

My parents gather closer to my bed, as if they're shielding me with their bodies. I have a sinking feeling I'm not going to like what they have to say.

"Simon," Dad begins, "we've been trying to talk to you, but we haven't managed to say the words, and I'm not sure now is the best time to get into it . . ."

"To get into it? Get into what?" I'm almost shouting, but I don't care. I'm already in the hospital.

What's the worst that can happen?

"Well, now that we know you're okay, maybe you're strong enough to hear the news," says Mom carefully. She and Dad exchange silent looks again, but somehow they've come to an agreement. "Your father and I have decided to separate." Mom delivers the news swiftly and frankly, as if ripping off a Band-Aid.

"What do you mean?" I stutter. "You're here, together, with me. You hugged. You have a family—a son and even a dog. Remember me?"

"Simon, we haven't been happy for so long. I know this will be a hard change, but it's for the best."

"No!" I shout. "No! Just try harder. Fix things! Don't do this to me."

By now I'm sobbing and I don't care. I just can't keep it together anymore. What was the point of it all? Of trying so hard to get an A in everything? Humiliating myself over and over again on social media? Hurting my friend? Getting beaten up?

Right now, I don't care about the VG Championships. I never want to play video games again.

I'd give up playing video games if it meant keeping my family together.

"Shhh," says Mom again. She winds her finger through my curly hair while Dad pats my leg.

"Did we really have to tell him this now, while he's still recovering?" Dad asks Mom.

"There's never going to be a good time to tell him," she says. "It's probably best that he hears the news while he's still under medical observation. Anyway, I think it's finally time for us to be honest with him."

"Yeah," says Dad, sadly. "It's not like he hasn't seen us fighting all this time."

Get out! I want to shout. *Get out!* I'm so confused. They're cooperating now while they're telling me they're splitting up! I keep crying and crying until my neck is wet and my eyes feel puffy. I stop myself from shouting at them—I feel so upset and afraid, and I realize this might be the last time we're all together as a family. I know that once we leave this hospital, nothing will ever be the same again.

Chapter 20

Eventually I got out of the hospital and went home to recover for a few weeks. You can never be too careful with brain injuries, my paediatrician said. Mom agreed. My parents made me stay home in bed, and they tended to me day and night. Mom and Dad even agreed on some things—namely that while I was still recovering from my concussion, I wasn't allowed to watch TV, play video games, or make videos for school. I didn't have to do any other homework—and for those few weeks, my parents didn't fight. I finally went back to school once my doctor gave the all clear.

Soon after, once she felt certain I'd recovered, Mom

found an apartment and moved out. At first, I was devastated that things went that way, especially when I realized that getting my parents to the VG Championships in Vancouver wasn't going to make them fall in love with each other again. Even though I knew they hadn't been getting along for ages, everything seemed to change quickly once they split up.

It hasn't been easy, but at least it's peaceful in the house now. Meg sleeps in my room, at the foot of my bed, a lot more these days. Mom still comes by the house to check on me every day. Both my parents seem happier—they can be in the same room without fighting. No more stomping and shouting and slamming doors.

It's a cold, grey day in December and the semester is almost over. Mr. Sayo is about to reveal the winner of the one and only A in tech class.

At this point, I couldn't care less if it's me. I look around the room at all my friends—friends who used social media to protect me, and each other, from bullying. My eyes flicker over the two empty seats vacated by the twins. Since they've been expelled and grounded, nobody at school or in the neighbourhood has seen or heard from them. The twins' VideoKids accounts have been removed from the server. It's like they never even existed.

The school has had several assemblies about bullying over the last two months, so we've been learning more about how to stop it and how not to be a passive bystander—that's when people see an incident and don't do anything about it. We even did a workshop in our Grade 7 homeroom class about something called restorative justice, which is supposed to help rebuild the relationship between bullies and their victims. I heard from my parents that Owen and Jeffrey are doing the restorative justice program, too, which means they might come back to school next year. If they do, maybe things won't be as bad as they once were.

As far as the VideoKids project goes: I think Jocelyn deserves the A more than anyone else in class. She always did. In fact, if I get the A, I'll ask Mr. Sayo to give it to her. Now that my parents are officially separated, I don't need it anymore. I have to accept that this is the new normal.

"Attention, attention!" Mr. Sayo is holding up his hands at the front of the class. The smile has returned to his face. I can't help but feel a little nervous. I cross my fingers and toes, hoping that Jocelyn is announced as the winner of the single A.

"Class, this has been a very interesting semester," Mr. Sayo says, once he has our attention. He makes eye contact with each and every one of us. His eyes hold mine for a second longer than is comfortable before he moves on to Jocelyn.

"We began in September by posing the question: What is engaging content? You all had a different response. Some of you posted videos about MMA, while others gained likes with Scrabble videos or interviews with interesting elderly people. Yet others learned to laugh at themselves by posting hilarious home videos. You all grew a loyal audience along the way."

"So who has the A?" yells Patrick, who can finally sit down again without the cushioning of the inflatable donut seat one of his elderly friends had loaned him while he was recovering from his bruised tailbone.

"I'll come to that soon," Mr. Sayo promises. He gets back to his original train of thought. "I'd like to say that this assignment turned into something so much more than creating engaging content. You learned to work together, to rise up, to use social media for the greater good. You found a way to empower yourselves, and in this way, you've prepared yourselves to be responsible citizens of the future—citizens who know how to use your power to protect each other. I'm proud of you all."

"Who got the A?" shouts Vivian.

We are all on the edge of our seats. Mr. Sayo chuckles.

"It is with great pride that I announce a change to the grading system. After everything you've accomplished together, I spoke to our friends at VideoKids. We have agreed that each and every one of you has earned an A, with the exception of one student."

Loud murmurs fill the room. If we all got an A, who is the one person who didn't?

A knock shifts our attention to the door. It's Mr. Burnstein again. Mr. Sayo waves him in.

"Hello class," says Mr. Burnstein, poking his head into the room. "I'm sorry to interrupt, but I have some news. Is this a good time?"

We all shout in unison. "No!"

Despite our collective response, Mr. Burnstein strides toward the centre of the room and stands beside Mr. Sayo. He smiles at us, ignoring our impatience. We want to get back to Mr. Sayo's announcement.

"I can tell from the excitement in the room that you've all learned your grade."

"With the exception of one student," Mr. Sayo corrects.

"So this *is* good timing, then," says Mr. Burnstein.

"Tell us!" someone shouts. That someone is me.

"Jocelyn, please come to the front of the room," says Mr. Burnstein.

Jocelyn and I lock eyes as she gets to her feet. She looks worried. I feel worried. I want to stand up and shout out. It's not fair. She shouldn't get a worse grade than us. If we all got As, how could Jocelyn be in trouble after all she did? I'm about to stand up and object when Mr. Burnstein finally continues.

"There is one student in the class who rose up and taught us all about what it means to be strong. This individual was a mighty friend. A friend who helped others, even if it meant making personal sacrifices. This person understood the true importance of this project and worked hard to collaborate with others for the greater good of the student body."

As I look around the room, I can't help but notice everyone is anxious. Some kids are biting their nails, while others are jiggling their legs or tapping their pencils against the desk. Patrick is sitting so close to the edge of his seat he could easily slide off.

"I'm proud to tell you that Jocelyn has earned an A+ in this class, as well as an MMA scholarship at her dojo, Combat Club."

The class erupts in applause.

Mr. Burnstein holds up his hands to quiet us down. "Not only that: Jocelyn's self-defence videos have generated so many views that her VideoKids channel has become profitable."

He smiles at Jocelyn and shakes her hand. Jocelyn is so

happy she's practically glowing. If she had the ability to levitate, that's what she'd be doing right now. Jocelyn faces the class and gives us a little show: a few quick jabs and kicks to the air. We all clap louder. Jocelyn got an A+. An MMA scholarship. A chance to earn some money. This is more than she could ever have hoped for. More than her parents would have dreamed.

We all pop up out of our seats to give Jocelyn a standing ovation. I whistle as loud as I can. Others shout "Woohoo!" Vivian gets up and waves her handmade scarf around like a lasso.

As I cheer with everyone else, I know in my heart this couldn't have happened to a better friend.

Chapter 21

I t's Christmas break, and I'm sitting in my room. Meg's chewing on a dirty pair of socks under my desk. Since finding some low-calorie treats at the pet store, Meg and I are back on good terms. I reach into the bag of "Bacon Bite-ettes" and feed her a couple. I don't have any videos to make now that tech class is over. I don't feel like playing video games.

Jocelyn's parents surprised her and her brother, Timothy, with a trip to Great Wolf Lodge. They love water parks, so it was the perfect Christmas gift. They had a lot to celebrate this year.

Jocelyn emailed to tell me they're having a great time.

She signed it *xox, Jocelyn*. Maybe there is a possibility of a kiss—a real one this time.

My phone rings, breaking the silence. It's Grandpa calling on FaceTime. I swipe right.

"Hi, Grandpa," I say as his image appears on screen.

"Whatcha doing?"

"Nothing," I say, sounding as down as I feel. No point in trying to hide it.

"You don't sound happy."

"I'm fine," I sigh.

"I know how I can cheer you up."

"I don't think that's possible, Grandpa, but thanks."

"Barbara, come here! Simon's on the phone!"

I turn my head in case she's not wearing any clothes again. Once was more than enough.

"Simon, honey!"

I peek at the screen. She's wearing clothes. I sigh in relief.

"Hi," I say with a wave.

"Grandpa and I have great news." Her eyes crinkle in the corners as she smiles.

"What?" I say, though nothing they can say will lift my mood.

"We know you've had a rough semester and that things at home are hard, too," says Grandma.

I roll my eyes. That's the understatement of the year.

"So Grandma and I are bringing you to Florida with us on the weekend!" finishes Grandpa.

"And guess what?" adds Grandma before I even have a chance to react. "You'll be there during the American VG Championships. We contacted the organizers of the

U.S. event to see if we could get you a ticket to watch the Americans in action this year. We've made all the arrangements."

My face lights up. But then I remember: I want to be mad. To refuse to go. To sit in my room and be miserable. But I can't. This is great news.

"Really?" I ask. Sometimes things are too good to be true.

"Yes, really," they say in unison.

"Pack your bags," says Grandpa. "But don't bring any stained underwear, okay honey? Just clean ones."

Grandma chuckles. "I loved that episode!"

"Wh—? How'd you know about that?" I splutter. Those videos were for school only. Are they online for everyone now? Could things seriously get any worse?

"My whole mah-jongg group was talking about it," Grandma explains. "One of the women has a grandson in your class—Patrick, I think. She saw the videos and told me all about them. You're a star, Simon!"

"We're so proud of you!" laughs Grandpa. "I didn't know you were so funny."

"I'm glad you learned to laugh at yourself and to stick up for yourself," says Grandma. "You've made such good friends, too. You've come a long way, Simon."

"And look at that—you haven't scratched your nose raw in weeks," Grandpa adds. "You've overcome your nervous tic."

They're right. It's gone! I guess I have become more confident and self-assured over the last few months while I've recovered. I've made new friends. I'm slowly getting back into MMA—it turns out that I like it a lot, and not just because Jocelyn encouraged to me try it. I'd even say that despite what happened with the Mendelsons and my parents, this last semester wasn't so bad after all. I have a feeling that things are going to be okay, even if my parents are no longer together.

"Thanks, Grandma and Grandpa."

"Get ready, Simon," says Grandpa. "We'll see you bright and early on Saturday."

I get up and do something I haven't done in weeks: a quick little floss dance. Meg bounds into my room and barks happily.

"That's right, Meg!" I tell her. "Let the games begin!"

Acknowledgments

Thank you to my family for their support and encouragement through every draft of this book, particularly my parents, my husband, my best friend and all my little beta readers (D, K, Z, L and M). Early readers who helped shape this book include Ruth Walker, Richard Scrimger and Ali MacDonald. I also want to thank Brian Henry, Dawn, Sarah and the rest of my Friday critique group for their ongoing feedback. All of these people have made every draft better than the last. And to Kirsten Marion and Common Deer Press for the opportunity to have this book published. I hope readers will laugh 'til they cry and that the story means something to children, especially those affected by divorce.

About the Author

Erin Silver has a postgraduate journalism degree and an MFA in Creative Nonfiction. She has been writing professionally for more than fifteen years. Her work has appeared in everything from *The Washington Post* and *Globe and Mail* to *Harper's Bazaar* and *Good Housekeeping*, among many other North American magazines, newspapers and blogs. One of her picture books was named a finalist in the 2017 CANSCAIP Writing for Children Competition and another was long listed in 2019. Her non-fiction children's book, *Proud to Play*, was published by Lorimer Children & Teens. Visit her at erinsilver.ca.